Run For Your Death . . .

As he reached the corner and started across, three men stepped from a doorway and grabbed hold of him. Two held his arms while the other moved around in front of him.

These men were going to hurt him.

Blindly he kicked out and caught the man in the midsection. With more strength than he would have ever thought he possessed, he pulled away from the two men holding him and began swinging wildly. Suddenly, he realized that instead of standing and fighting he should be running, and he ran, trying to get away, waiting for a shot to ring out, waiting for a bullet to strike him in the back. . . .

Also in THE GUNSMITH series

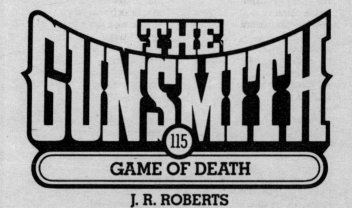

THE GUNSMITH

115

GAME OF DEATH

J. R. ROBERTS

JOVE BOOKS, NEW YORK

GAME OF DEATH

A Jove Book / published by arrangement with
the author

PRINTING HISTORY
Jove edition / July 1991

ISBN: 0-515-10615-1

Jove Books are published by The Berkley Publishing Group,
200 Madison Avenue, New York, New York 10016.
The name "JOVE" and the "J" logo
are trademarks belonging to Jove Publications, Inc.

PRINTED IN THE UNITED STATES OF AMERICA

10 9 8 7 6 5 4 3 2 1

PROLOGUE

Clint Adams had only ever seen one baseball game in his life, and that was when he was in New York City. When he heard that there was going to be a baseball game in Kansas, just ten miles from where he was, he decided to go and see it.

Clint was in a little town called Shetland, Kansas. He read in the *Shetland Inquirer* that there was to be a baseball "exhibition" in nearby Hutchinson in two days' time.

"Well, what do you know about that?"

"Hmmm?" the girl next to him in bed said. "About what, Clint?"

"There's going to be a baseball game in Hutchinson." Clint looked at her and said, "That's about ten miles from here, isn't it?"

"Hmm? Yeah, about ten miles."

He looked at the newspaper and then back down at the girl. She had the sheet pulled up to her neck, but he could see the outline of one rounded shoulder against it. The only other thing he could see was the top of her blond head.

He frowned, trying to remember her name.

"Kate?"

She didn't move.

He tried again.

"Kelly?"

No response.

Last night had been unusual. He had drank more than usual, and when he had come back here with the girl he was more than a little inebriated. Consequently, he was having a hard time now remembering her name.

Wait a minute: It was something uncommon . . . starting with the letter *K* . . . no, not *K*, *C*. . . .

"Christine?"

"Hmm?"

Success.

He slid his hand beneath the sheet and found her hip. It was smooth, warm, and slender. It was coming back to him now. She was a tall, high-breasted blonde with a slim waist and hips and long legs that seemed to go on forever. He remembered her wrapping those legs around his waist and being surprised by how strong she was.

"Mmmm."

He moved his hand to the outside of her thigh, then around to the inside. She moved her legs so he could slide his hand between them, and then she closed her thighs on him.

"You awake?" he asked.

"Almost," she said from beneath the sheet. "Keep trying."

He moved his hand up until he felt her coarse pubic hair. He found the smooth lips of her pussy and ran his finger along them, moistening them.

"Now?"

"Almost there . . ."

She moved again, spreading her legs, and he dipped his finger inside of her.

"Now," she said, rolling onto her back and opening her legs wide, "I'm awake!"

"Clint?" Christine said about a half an hour later.

"Huh?"

"What's baseball?"

Clint entered the saloon and walked right up to the bar. He'd been in Shetland for three days—long enough for the bartender to know that he wanted a beer when he came to the saloon. He'd only been passing through, but he found Shetland to be a friendly town, and it offered him some gunsmithing business. He hadn't met Christine until last night, his third night in town.

"You look tired," Ben, the bartender, said as he set the beer down in front of Clint.

"Yeah."

"Long night with Christine?" the man asked, wiggling his eyebrows.

"Long morning."

"The morning, too?"

Clint took a sip of beer. "I spent most of the morning trying to explain baseball to her. There's going to be a game in Hutchinson day after tomorrow."

"Baseball?" Ben said, frowning. "What's that?"

"It's a game played with a bat and a ball. One man throws the ball and another man tries to hit it with the bat. Is that clear to you?"

"Sure," Ben said, "except for one thing."

"What's that?"

"What's a bat?"

Clint gave the man a baleful glare. "Never mind."

"Are you planning on going to see this . . . batball game?"

"It's *base*ball," Clint said, "and yes, I was thinking about it. I think I've been here long enough, anyway. Time to move on."

"You know, sometimes I think about that," Ben said.

"About what?"

"Traveling, drifting—you know, the way you do. Must be a great life. Different towns, different women . . ."

"Why don't you do it?"

"Nah," Ben said, "my wife would never let me."

"Well, that's one thing you don't have to worry about when you live a life like mine," Clint said. "Having a wife."

He wasn't only referring to the fact that he traveled, but to the violent part of his life—which had always been the biggest part. There was no room for a woman who might catch a bullet meant for the Gunsmith.

"When will you be leaving?" Ben asked.

"In the morning," Clint said. He finished his beer and said, "See you later. I want to check my rig and team and make sure they'll be ready to travel."

Ben watched as Clint Adams walked out of the saloon, then picked up his empty beer mug. Shetland had been pretty excited about having the Gunsmith in town. The townspeople had also been surprised to find out how nice a man Clint Adams was. When a man had a reputation like his, he was usually arrogant, but not Clint Adams.

Ben wondered what it would be like to have a man like Clint Adams settle in a town like Shetland.

He wondered how many times Clint Adams might have wondered the same thing.

ONE

Baseball made its first appearance just after the Civil War, when the Cincinnati Red Stockings made their debut as baseball's first professional team. Shortly thereafter, in 1876, the National League was formed.

Clint Adams didn't know any of this when he rode into Hutchinson, Kansas. All he knew was that a baseball team from the east had been touring the west, and it was stopping over in Kansas before returning home.

There was something else he didn't know: The Cedar Rapids Bulls were trying to gain entry into the National League. The tour of the west was just a way of keeping in shape until the baseball season started back east. When they returned to Cedar Rapids, they were supposed to have a series of games against National League teams, the outcome of which would determine whether or not they would be allowed into the league.

It was the job of Manager Doug DeWitt, who also played first base, to get his team into shape for the series. He had thirty men traveling with him. Since there were no baseball

teams in the west, professional or otherwise, they basically squared off against each other. It didn't matter which
side won, as long as they played hard and executed their
plays well.

They arrived in Hutchinson two days early. They had to
find a field large enough to play in and then measure out
the distances for the bases, pitcher's mound and home plate.
The team carried three extra men to set the field up and
make sure it was playable and three more men to umpire
the games. Thirty-six men in all, traveling in eight wagons,
and it was Doug DeWitt's job to make sure that his men
were ready to play. That meant trying to keep them out of
saloons and away from women, which was a big job for
one man.

Doug DeWitt was forty years old, and he knew his days
as a baseball player were numbered. He was six feet tall and
still had good hands, but he was starting to thicken around
the middle and his foot speed was not what it had once
been. Also, he was having some trouble seeing the ball of
late, and he suspected that his eyesight was starting to fail.
As he watched the field being set up, he wondered what the
hell he was doing out here, playing nursemaid to a bunch
of overgrown little boys, most of whom would rather slide
into a cheap woman than first base.

Ted Banner walked over and stood next to DeWitt. He
was in charge of finding the areas where they would set
up a field and making sure the field was playable. He also
served as a coach. Banner was in his forties, a gangly man
with very big hands and feet.

"Well?" DeWitt asked.

"It'll do," Banner said.

"I don't want my men getting killed by a bad hop when
the ball hits a hole, Ted."

"We're filling in the holes, Doug. Don't worry."

"I'm counting on you," DeWitt said. "Sammy's still not talking right since that ball hit him in the throat."

"Don't worry, Doug."

"Just check it and check it again," DeWitt said. "I've got to go to town and find my players. Most of them will probably be drunk, or in bed with a whore."

Banner didn't say anything. He himself had gotten drunk the night before and spent that night with a whore.

"Good luck."

"Yeah," DeWitt said, scowling. "I'm gonna need it."

Keith Cosner was the star pitcher of the Cedar Rapids Bulls. He'd spent one season with the Cincinnati Red Stockings, but he had injured his arm halfway through the season and had only just gotten his arm back into shape. He was now sure that he was once again the pitcher he had been for the Red Stockings, when he'd won fifteen games before being injured.

He had tried to get his spot back with the Red Stockings, but they'd claimed they didn't need him anymore. He had then gone to some of the other National League teams, but all claimed they had no room on their rosters for him. It was then that he managed to latch on with the Bulls. They were pleased to have a former professional pitcher on their team, because they were looking to *become* a professional team. What they hadn't counted on was the fact that Cosner was so arrogant that every other player on the team hated him—which had also been the case when he'd been with the Red Stockings. That was the real reason that the Stockings and the other professional teams hadn't wanted him—that and the fact that they all considered him to be damaged goods. He intended to prove them wrong, and the humbling experience of the past couple of years— there had been times when he couldn't even lift his arm— had done nothing to dim his arrogance.

It was all Doug DeWitt could do to keep his teammates from tarring and feathering Cosner, but DeWitt was convinced they'd never make it into the National League without him.

DeWitt drove his rented buggy back into Hutchinson, hoping that he'd find most of his players still asleep at the hotel or having lunch somewhere. If they'd been out late enough the night before, chances were good that they hadn't yet awakened.

He stopped the buggy in front of the hotel, where his players were packed four and five a room because there were so many of them. DeWitt himself was the only one who was sharing a room with only one other person, and that was Ted Banner. He knew that Banner had come in late last night, but that old bugger seemed to be able to outdrink and outwhore any player on the team, even those twenty years younger than he was.

DeWitt entered the hotel and checked the dining room first. Sure enough, five of his players were seated at a table, packing in the chow.

"Hey, Doug," one of them shouted. "Come on and fall to. There's plenty of food."

DeWitt approached the table.

"I already ate, thanks. I'm here to tell you fellers to stay out of trouble today and get in early tonight. We're playing tomorrow."

"Aw, shoot," one of the younger players said. "We're only playin' each other. What's the problem? We'll put on a good show for the folks."

"These folks have never seen a baseball game in their lives, Ory," DeWitt said. "I want them to see a damned good one. Besides, this is our last one before we head back to Iowa."

"And the National League!" one of them shouted, and the other chimed in with cheers.

"All right, all right, keep it down," DeWitt said. The other diners were staring at them. "The rest of the boys upstairs?"

"I guess so," Clyde James said. He was one of the older players and, supposedly, a steadying influence on the others. "We ain't seen any of them leave since we got here. Course, some of them coulda left before we got up and we wouldn't know it."

"I'll check the rooms," DeWitt said.

"Doug?"

"Yeah, Ory?" Ory Sather was one of the youngest players on the team, still young enough to feel he had to tell his manager everything he knew.

"I saw Keith leavin' the hotel just as we was comin' down the steps."

"That figures," said DeWitt, as Clyde James made a disgusted face at the younger player. "Was he alone, Ory?"

"Uh, no," Ory said, fidgeting now under the collective gaze of the other players. They had no love for Cosner, but he was still one of the team, and you didn't talk to the manager about one of the team. Ory Sather hadn't learned that lesson yet. "He had Jerry Cole with him."

"That's great," DeWitt said. "Not bad enough that Cosner's trying to wreck his own career, but he's got to take Jerry down with him."

"How much trouble could he get into this early, Skipper?" James asked DeWitt.

"I don't know, Clyde," DeWitt said, "but I guess it's my job to find out, ain't it? I'll do that right after I check on the rest of the boys."

TWO

Clint Adams had felt a small tingle of excitement as he rode up on some men who were measuring out the distances for the baseball diamond in a field just outside of town. He had watched them for a few minutes and then ridden into town.

Riding down the main street of Hutchinson, he saw posters stuck to walls and poles announcing the baseball game, which was to be played the following morning.

He directed his team to the livery, where he arranged to put up the rig and team and Duke, his big black gelding. Liverymen were usually a little put out at having to give up so much room to him, but they usually felt differently when he walked them around to the back of the wagon and showed them Duke.

This one was no different.

"That there's a beautiful animal, mister."

"I know it," Clint said. "I hope I'm putting him in good hands."

"The best hands in the state, mister," the liveryman replied.

"You betcha." The man was in his fifties, and he had the gnarled, oft-bitten hands of a man who had handled horses for a lot of years.

They settled on a price for the rig and three horses, and then Clint took his saddlebags and headed for the hotel. As he entered, he heard a commotion of voices from the dining room, and then he saw a thick, fortyish man come walking out while the noise behind him died down. As the man went up the stairs to his right, Clint walked to the desk and told the clerk he needed a room.

"Yessir."

"The baseball players have rooms here?"

The clerk gave him a quick look. "Yessir, but they're a . . . well, not too noisy."

"Is that them in the dining room?"

The clerk winced. "Yessir, but—"

"Relax, mister," Clint said. "I ain't the complaining type. Just give me a room."

Clint signed in, collected his key, inquired about a bath, and then made arrangements for one within the next half-hour.

As he went up the steps, he passed the same man who had come out of the dining room. The man was scowling, in an obvious hurry, but as Clint moved over to one side the man still had the courtesy to say "Excuse me" as he squeezed by.

"Sure," Clint said, and he continued on up.

Doug DeWitt was not a happy man.

He'd checked on his other players and had found most of them still sleeping. In fact, only two—other than the men in the dining room—were not in their rooms: Keith Cosner and Jerry Cole.

Cole was a young shortstop with a lot of potential, but he had fallen under the spell of the hard-living Cosner.

DeWitt couldn't understand Cosner. The man was looking desperately for a second chance in baseball, but that didn't cause him to modify the way in which he lived. He still did more drinking and whoring than any other two men on the team. Cosner's talent was God given, and he was doing his best to destroy it.

DeWitt squeezed by the stranger who had just registered and left the hotel, heading for the whorehouse.

Clint enjoyed his bath and went into the dining room to look for some lunch. The rowdy bunch of ballplayers had long since left, but their presence wouldn't have bothered Clint. He was looking forward to seeing the game, and he wouldn't have minded meeting some of the players while he ate.

Clint could see the lobby from his table while he was having his lunch. He saw the man he'd seen that morning come back into the hotel, pushing two younger men ahead of him. He could even hear their voices.

"Don't push, DeWitt," one of the men was saying. He was about twenty-eight or so, while the other young man couldn't have been more than twenty.

The man called DeWitt said, "I'll do more than push you, Cosner. You can destroy your own career, but Cole is just starting out."

Cosner turned on DeWitt. "Which is more than we can say for you, eh, Doug?"

DeWitt pointed a thick forefinger at Keith Cosner and said, "Don't try me, Cosner, because I'll break your pitching arm. Let me see you make a comeback with a busted wing!"

Clint watched as the younger man, Cosner, stood his ground for a few moments and then backed off. Clint assumed this meant that DeWitt would have broken his arm if it had come to that.

"Skip—" the other man began, but DeWitt cut him off savagely.

"You get up to your room, Cole!" he snapped. "I don't want to see you out of it until the game tomorrow."

THREE

Clint wandered over to the saloon after lunch and was surprised to find it so busy this early in the afternoon. He had only to stand at the bar for a few moments to discover that most of the men in the saloon were ballplayers.

There were three tables of them, about fourteen men in all, and for a group that large they were being surprisingly well behaved. The other men in the saloon, five or six at the most, didn't seem to like the players, though. They had banded together at one table and scowled at the Easterners who had invaded their territory.

Clint stood alone at the bar, watching in the mirror the tableau forming behind him.

The six men all seemed to be from town. None of them were particularly dressed as cowpunchers, so he assumed they were not from a nearby ranch. They all wore guns, however, while not one of the ballplayers was armed.

The ballplayers were all laughing and having a good time, and the two saloon girls who were working that early were floating among the three tables.

The six townspeople didn't like that, either.

Clint knew that something was going to give soon, and he stood ready to step in if gunplay developed.

"Hey, Rachel!" one of the townsmen shouted. "What's the matter, you like Easterners better than us?"

Rachel, a tall, busty, black-haired gal, looked over at the table of six and said, "I do when they're better behaved than you, Wally Oxman."

"Better behaved?" Oxman shouted drunkenly. The six townsmen had been consuming more whiskey than the fourteen ballplayers. "Whataya mean, better behaved? We're behavin', ain't we, boys?"

"We sure are," the others agreed, nodding.

"Come on, Rachel," one of them said, "bring your pretty self over here."

Rachel dismissed them with a wave of her hand and continued talking to the ballplayers.

"Kathy," Oxman shouted at the other girl. She was blond, as tall as Rachel but built along leaner lines.

She also dismissed Oxman and his bunch with a wave of her hand.

"Hey!" Oxman shouted, standing up.

"Take it easy, Wally," the bartender said.

The bartender was a tall, thin, dark-haired man with a nervous manner. He was busy polishing the hell out of the same glass as he watched what was developing.

"Don't tell me to take it easy, Del," Oxman said. "You keep out of this."

The bartender frowned and looked at Clint.

"Is he hotheaded enough to use that gun he's wearing?" Clint asked.

"He is," the bartender said nervously.

"You'd better go and get the sheriff then," Clint said.

"Yessir," Del said. "I guess I had better." He put the glass down and eased out from behind the bar.

"Stand up," Oxman said, and his friends obeyed.

"Hey, you Easterners!" Oxman shouted. "You . . . you . . . ballplayers!"

One of the ballplayers looked over and said, "Are you talking to us?"

"Damned right, I am! Them's our women you're talking to."

The Easterners looked at Rachel and Kathy, and one of them asked, "Are you their women?"

"Heck, no," Rachel said.

"I guess they ain't," the ballplayer said to Oxman, and he looked away.

Oxman viciously kicked his chair away and said, "Don't you look away from me, boy."

He was tense, one hand poised above his gun.

The ballplayers seemed to realize all of a sudden that they weren't armed and the other six men were.

"Now wait a minute," one of them said.

Oxman pointed at the spokesman and said, "You ain't got a gun."

"N-no," the man said, "I don't."

Rachel and Kathy had backed away from the ballplayers now and were watching from across the room.

"Don't worry about that," Oxman said, grinning. "I'll give you one."

"I—I don't know how to use a gun," the man said.

"That's your problem," Oxman said. He turned to one of his friends. "Gimme a gun." When Oxman had another gun in his hand, he said, "You boys better find one of you who does know how to use a gun, and quick."

The ballplayers began exchanging glances, and it was soon clear that none of them was proficient enough with a gun to face Oxman.

"All right then," Oxman said, "I'll pick one."

Clint turned around, wondering where the hell the sheriff was. "Hold on, friend," he said.

Oxman looked over at Clint and frowned.

"You ain't no Easterner," he said.

"No, I'm not."

"Then mind your own business."

"I can't do that."

"Why not?"

"Because you're talking too loud for me to do that," Clint said.

"You sayin' I got a big mouth?" Oxman asked.

"I guess that's what I'm saying," Clint said. "Now why don't you and your friends just leave these boys alone and be on your way."

Oxman turned to face Clint squarely. "You takin' their side, stranger?"

"I'm taking my side, friend," Clint said. "I was having a nice quiet drink and then you started yelling. I'm telling you to leave."

"You're *tellin'* me to leave?"

"That's right."

Oxman turned and handed the extra gun back to its owner.

"You figure you can face six of us, friend?" Oxman asked, grinning drunkenly.

"I figure the six of you are drunk enough to give me a good chance," Clint said. "Even if I can't take the six of you, I'll take you first, friend."

"You'll be dead soon after."

"You won't live long enough to see it," Clint said. "Now, the call is up to you. Make it."

Oxman stared at Clint for a long moment, licking his lips. The men behind him began to fidget and exchange glances. For a man facing six guns, Clint was too calm to suit them.

"Wally . . ." one of them began.

"Quiet," Oxman said. "We ain't backin' down from one man."

A couple of his friends exchanged glances, and then one of them said, "Maybe you ain't backin' down, but we are. Fun is fun, but this is gettin' too serious. Come on, boys."

Oxman turned and watched as three men peeled off and left the saloon.

"Cowards!" he shouted.

"They aren't cowards, Oxman," Clint said. "They're just smart enough to know that there isn't anything here worth dying for. You should be as smart."

"There's still three of us," Oxman said, wetting his lips again.

"Do it, then," Clint said. "Go ahead. I haven't killed anyone all week."

The line sounded comical even to him, but Oxman was drunk enough to miss its comical aspect.

"Shit," Oxman said.

"Wally . . ." one of his friends said.

"Shit," Oxman said again. "Let's get out of here."

Oxman and his two remaining friends left, and Clint turned to finished his beer.

FOUR

Clint was still drinking his beer when one of the ball-players came up to the bar and stood beside him.

"We'd like to thank you for what you did," the man said. "Those fellers might have killed us."

"Well, I couldn't very well let that happen, now, could I?" Clint asked. "Not when I came here to see you boys play."

"Really?" the man asked. "You came to see us play?"

"That's right."

The man stuck out his hand and said, "My name's Sam Malone. I'd like to ask you to join us, mister."

Clint took the man's hand. "My name is Clint Adams, and I'd like to do that."

Malone was a tall, open-faced, blond man in his mid-twenties, and he had himself a good grip.

"Come on over and meet the rest of the fellers," Malone invited.

As Clint picked up his beer to do so, the batwing doors opened and the bartender came back in, trailing the sheriff behind him.

"What the hell are you talkin' about, Del?" the sheriff demanded. "I don't see no hint of trouble."

"There was some trouble, Sheriff," Sam Malone said, "but this feller here took care of it."

"Is that a fact?" the lawman asked. He was a full-bellied man in his late forties, with a huge mustache and bushy eyebrows.

"It sure is," one of the other ballplayers chimed in. "He stood off six gunmen and made them back down."

"He did that, eh?"

"They weren't exactly gunmen, Sheriff," Clint said. "Just some of your townspeople who got a little too drunk, is all."

"I see," the lawman said, as Del moved back around behind the bar. "And what might your name be, stranger?"

"Adams," Clint said. "Clint Adams, Sheriff. I just arrived in town today to watch the baseball game that's scheduled for tomorrow."

The sheriff was staring at Clint in a way that made Clint know that the man recognized his name.

"Uh-huh," the sheriff said. "Well, Mr. Adams, you enjoy the game now, hear?"

"Sure, Sheriff."

The lawman gave the bartender a hard stare, then smiled nervously at Clint and backed out of the saloon.

"Now, what do you suppose made the sheriff so nervous all of a sudden?" Sam Malone asked.

Clint shrugged. "He must be the nervous type, I guess. That invitation to join you boys still open?"

"It sure is," Malone said enthusiastically. "And the drinks are on us!"

For the rest of the afternoon, Clint drank and talked with the fourteen ballplayers. They wanted to know about him and about the West, while he wanted to know about them and baseball. He was getting his way for most of the afternoon, learning about the game and finding out what position each played. Finally, one of the players went to the bar for some beers and asked the bartender if he knew who Clint was.

"You mean you don't know who you been drinking with?" the bartender asked.

"No, sir. Is he someone important?"

"Important?" the bartender repeated. "*Dangerous* is more like it. Why, son, that there is the Gunsmith."

"The Gunsmith?"

"You don't know who the Gunsmith is?"

"I'm sorry," the player said, "I don't."

"Why, son, he's only the fastest gun since Wild Bill Hickok—and some say he was faster than Bill himself."

The name Hickok rang a bell with the player. He was a child when Hickok had come to St. Louis to do some stage work. His father had told him all about Wild Bill Hickok, so to learn that the man who had been drinking with them all afternoon might have been faster than Wild Bill was as exciting as hell.

He grabbed two handfuls of beer mugs and hurried back to the table to tell his friends.

FIVE

When the man returned from the bar Clint sensed the excitement in him, and he could guess why. He looked over at the bartender, Del, who turned and looked away.

"Well, boys," the man said, "we got a real celebrity among us."

"Who's that, Cool?" Sam Malone asked. "You?"

"No," George Cool said, "him." He pointed at Clint.

"Clint Adams?" Malone asked. He looked at Clint. "Are you a celebrity, Clint?"

"Your friend Mr. Cool is telling it," Clint said. "What did you find out, Mr. Cool?"

Cool looked nervous all of a sudden, but he spoke up anyway.

"According to the bartender, Mr. Adams is the fastest gun since Wild Bill Hickok."

"Who's Wild Bill Hickok?" one young man of about twenty asked, but the others ignored him.

"Faster than Hickok?" Malone repeated. "Is that true, Clint?"

"No."

"No?"

"The fastest *since* Hickok?" Cool asked.

"Don't ask me," Clint said. "I haven't timed everyone in the West yet. I'm still working on Texas."

"I get the feeling you're being a little modest here, Clint," Malone said. The other players started asking questions simultaneously, and Malone held his hands up and waved them off.

"I'll talk for everyone," he said to the other players, and then he addressed himself to Clint. "Let's say it straight, Clint: Are you good with a gun?"

"Yes."

"Very good?"

"Yes."

"As good as—"

"I thought we were saying it straight," Clint said.

"All right," Malone said, smiling. "Do you have a reputation with a gun?"

"Yes."

"They call him the Gunsmith," George Cool spoke up.

"The Gunsmith!" Malone said. "I've heard that name, even back east. You're the Gunsmith?"

"Some people call me that, yes."

"Well," Malone said, "I'll be damned."

"He is a celebrity," Cool said, smiling, and the others started talking again.

"Settle down," Malone said.

"How fast can you draw your gun?" one of the players asked.

"How fast can you throw a ball?"

"Sam's the pitcher," Cool said.

"Number two on the team," Malone admitted.

"Who's number one?" Clint asked.

"Keith Cosner," Malone said, and some of the other players moaned.

"I take it this Cosner is not popular."

"He's got an ego this big," Malone said, spreading his hands wide.

"Why?"

"Because he's good," Malone said. "What about you?"

"What about me?"

"Do you have an ego because you're good?"

"I don't think so."

"Well, Keith does," one player said.

"He was in the National League once," another man said.

"The National League?"

"That's the professional league," Malone said. "We're trying to get in, and Keith might be our ticket."

"Sam's twice the pitcher Keith is," George Cool said. Some of the men voiced their agreement, and some of them abstained.

"That remains to be seen," Malone said.

"No ego?" Clint asked.

"Oh, I've got an ego," Malone said. "I know I'm good, but I'm not sure I'm better than Keith."

"That's all you need," Clint said. "To know you're good."

"Is that what you know?" Malone asked. "That you're good?"

"Good enough."

"For what?"

"To still be alive."

Malone sat back as the other players waited for him to say something. It seemed they had finally agreed that he would be the sole spokesman.

"You know what I think?" Malone asked.

"What?"

"I think we have a lot in common."

"Like what?"

"What we do."

"You pitch," Clint said. "What do I do?"

"I mean I pitch and you shoot a gun—accurately."

"And do you throw a ball accurately?"

"Yes," Malone said. "You know, if we had the time, I'd say we could teach each other."

"Why would you want to learn to shoot a gun?" Clint asked. "And why would I want to learn how to throw a ball?"

"Not throw a ball," Malone corrected, "pitch a ball."

"What's the difference?"

"Is there somewhere I can show you?"

"Sure," Clint said. "There's usually an alley behind a saloon. Let's take a look."

They all got up and milled about while Clint turned to the bartender.

"Hey, Del?"

"Yeah?"

"Where's the back door?"

"Through there," Del said, pointing to a curtained doorway.

"Is there an alley back there?"

"Sure."

Clint turned to the fourteen ballplayers and said, "Let's go."

SIX

There was indeed an alley behind the saloon, and it was plenty long enough for their needs.

"The pitching mound is forty-five feet from the plate," Malone said. "Cool, mark it off."

George Cool walked off forty-five feet and drew something in the dirt. Clint assumed that it was supposed to be the "plate."

"What do we do now?" Clint asked.

"We're waiting," Malone said. "I sent one of the boys for some balls and gloves. Of course, you could show us some shooting while we're waiting."

"I don't do trick shooting."

"Why not?"

"A gun is not a toy," Clint said. "I draw it when I intend to use it."

"That why you didn't draw it on those six men?"

"There was no need."

"And if they had drawn?"

"Then I would have."

26

"Were you that confident that you could take the six of them?"

"I was that confident that I wouldn't have to."

"You took a big chance."

"Not so big," Clint said. "I've been through so many situations like that that I can usually tell when there's a real danger of gunplay."

"And there wasn't any today?"

"Not that I could see," Clint said.

"If there was no danger, then why did you step in?"

"There was no danger of them drawing on me," Clint said. "That didn't mean there wasn't danger of them drawing on you fellers."

"But . . . we were unarmed."

"And much less of a threat to them than I was," Clint said. "See what I mean?"

"I suppose I do."

"Here come the balls and gloves," someone shouted.

One of the players had come from the street and was carrying two leather gloves and some baseballs.

"Here," Malone said. He took one of the balls and tossed it to Clint, who caught it.

"Johnny, go and get into a crouch," Malone said.

Johnny Day ran forty-five feet down the alley and crouched down by the squarish figure drawn into the dirt.

"Throw the ball to him," Malone said.

Clint looked down the alley at Johnny Day and then tossed the ball to him. It fell ten feet short and rolled to the man.

"Try it again," Malone said. "Try to reach him this time."

Malone gave Clint another ball. Clint threw it to Johnny Day, and Day caught it over his head. Clint had thrown it too hard this time."

"You're throwing the ball," Malone said. "I'm going to pitch it."

Clint watched as Malone stared down at Johnny Day, then held the ball at his chest, reared back, and—and suddenly Johnny Day had the ball. Clint had not seen the ball go from Malone's hand to Day's glove, but he heard it strike the leather with a pop.

"That's pitching," one of the other men said.

"Do it again," Clint said.

"All right."

Clint watched closely this time, and he saw the ball go from Malone's hand to Day's glove. He was still impressed, but this time he'd been able to watch the flight of the ball.

"Do you think you can do that?" Malone asked. "Pitch, instead of throw?"

"I can try," Clint said.

Malone waved at Day, who threw all three of the balls back.

"Here," Malone said, handing Clint a ball. "Pitch it."

Clint had watched Malone extremely closely the second time. He'd noticed that when Malone held the ball he held it by the seams—that is, his index and middle fingers covered the seams of the ball. Clint held the ball that way, and he found it comfortable.

He did not try to imitate the movement of Malone's body. Instead, he concentrated on the glove Johnny Day was holding, and he threw ball . . . Hard. It made a popping sound as it struck the leather of the glove, and Johnny Day stood up and stared.

Clint turned to look at Sam Malone and found the man staring at him, as were all of the other players.

"What's wrong?"

Malone held another ball out to him and said, "Do it again."

Clint took the ball, held it the same way, and threw it to Day—or rather, "pitched" it. He still felt as if he were throwing the ball.

Once again it made the popping sound as it struck the glove, and Clint thought he saw Johnny Day wince.

"Two perfect strikes!" someone said in a hushed tone.

"And *fast*!" someone else said.

"Did I do something wrong?" Clint asked.

"Clint . . . have you ever thrown a baseball before?" Malone asked.

"No."

"Tell me the truth now," Malone said. "You've never thrown one before?"

Clint laughed. "I have never thrown a baseball before. I've never even held any kind of ball before. Now tell me what's going on."

Johnny Day came walking up to hear what was being said. He showed Sam Malone his hand, the palm of which was vivid red.

"Malone," Clint began.

"Clint," said Sam Malone, shaking his head as if he were in a daze, "you just threw two of the most perfect strikes I've ever seen—faster than I've ever seen. I don't know a man alive who would have been able to touch them with a bat."

"Not faster than you."

Malone laughed and said, "I'm afraid so. I wish I had your velocity."

"He even threw faster than Keith Cosner," Johnny Day said.

Clint gave Day a look, and Day said, "I catch both Cosner and Sam here, Clint, and neither of them has ever stung my hand the way you just did—twice."

"So," Clint said, shrugging his shoulders, "what does that mean?"

"Clint," Sam Malone said, a crafty look on his face, "how would you like to pitch for a professional baseball team?"

SEVEN

"This is crazy," Doug DeWitt said.

"That's what I told him," Clint said.

DeWitt looked across the table at Clint. "You're Clint Adams?"

"That's right."

"I've seen you before. . . . In the hotel lobby?"

"Right again."

"Look, Mr. Adams, if you want to play baseball—"

"Hey, hold it," Clint said, "I never said I wanted to play baseball."

"Well then, what's this all about?" DeWitt asked. He looked at Malone. "Why did you have me come over here?"

Johnny Day came over to the table and put a beer in front of DeWitt.

"Have a beer, Skip," he offered.

"I don't want a beer. What the hell is going on?"

"Look, Doug," Malone said, "Clint is very, very good with a gun."

"So what?" Clint noticed that Doug DeWitt was staring

at the beer, and then he abruptly pushed it away from him. Some of the beer sloshed over onto the table.

The other players had all gone off somewhere together, leaving it to Sam Malone and Johnny Day to try and talk Doug DeWitt into making Clint Adams an offer—*and* trying to talk Clint Adams into it as well.

Sam Malone leaned forward. "The same talents that make him good with a gun can make him a good pitcher," he said. "He's got a strong arm, a sharp eye, and deadly concentration."

"That's crazy," DeWitt said.

"See?" Clint said.

"Doug, come out back with us and watch for yourself. You'll see."

"Sam," Clint began.

"Clint, the Bulls are trying to get into the National League. Another pitcher—a pitcher like you could be— might be what we need to get us in."

"I'm too old," Clint said.

"He's too old," DeWitt agreed.

"He's not much older than you, Doug," Malone said, and DeWitt shut up.

"Clint," Malone asked, "will you throw the ball for Doug?"

Clint thought a moment, then said, "No . . . but I'll pitch it."

"Doug?" Malone looked at his manager.

DeWitt studied the three of them for a moment, then shrugged and said, "Hell, why not? I've got nothing better to do."

Clint, Sam Malone, Johnny Day, and Doug DeWitt all went into the alley behind the saloon. Day ran down by the makeshift home plate and crouched down.

"Watch," Malone said, tossing a ball to Clint.

Clint peered down at Day, saw where Day was holding the glove, and "pitched" the ball. *Pop*! It landed right in the center of the glove.

Doug DeWitt narrowed his eyes and said to Clint, "Let me see you do that again."

Smiling, Malone tossed Clint another ball, and Clint did it again.

Pop!

Johnny Day stood up, shaking his hand.

DeWitt looked at Malone and said, "He doesn't have the motion."

"I can teach him the pitching motion, Skip," Malone said. "That's no problem. Hell, if he winds up properly he might even pitch better."

"Well," DeWitt said, stroking his jaw and looking Clint up and down, "he does seem to have the raw talent—even if he is a little old."

"For baseball," Clint qualified.

"Right," DeWitt said, "for baseball. No offense meant, Mr. Adams."

"None taken, Mr. DeWitt."

"Whataya say, Skip?" Malone asked. "Give him a tryout. Let him play with us tomorrow."

DeWitt looked at Malone and said, "He's got to want to do it, Sam."

Malone looked at Clint.

"How about it, Clint?" he asked. "Want to play some ball tomorrow?"

"What will the other players think of this?" Clint asked. He couldn't believe that he was actually considering doing it. "A stranger coming in and playing on their team?"

"Hell," Malone said, "you met more than half the team here and they're all for it. They'll go along with whatever's good for the team." Malone knew that all of the men would, too. Except for Keith Cosner. "The others ain't worth a shit. Whataya say, Clint?"

Clint looked at Malone, then at DeWitt.

"What could it hurt?" DeWitt asked.

"Nothing, I guess," Clint said. "All right, I'll do it. I'll play ball."

When Doug DeWitt left the saloon he was excited. True, Clint Adams was older than most baseball players—himself included—but DeWitt knew a real prospect when he saw one. He only wished he'd found Clint Adams fifteen . . . ten . . . even five years ago. He wished he'd found a twenty-five-year old man with an arm like Clint Adams, instead of a middle-aged gunman.

There was no way in hell that Clint Adams had a baseball career ahead of him. Hell, from what Doug DeWitt had heard—and *he* had recognized Adam's name when Malone had first introduced them—the man's career was killing people.

All Doug DeWitt wanted from Clint Adams was one season. Just one. He needed him to be able to pitch the Cedar Rapids Bulls right into the National League. If he was going to get Adams to do that, he was going to have to play this just right.

As he hurried to his hotel room to figure out a plan, he wondered idly how Clint Adams would hit.

Malone and Johnny Day wanted to go back into the saloon to have a drink in celebration, but Clint begged off and left them in the saloon. Ahead of him he watched Doug DeWitt hurrying toward the hotel.

This was still crazy, he thought, but he felt a tingle of excitement. The one time he had seen a baseball game he had enjoyed it. Now he wondered what it would be like

to be a ballplayer and to have nothing to worry about but
playing a game.

He was looking forward to tomorrow, unaware that some
people had plans for him beyond that.

EIGHT

When Keith Cosner heard the news he was not shy about voicing his displeasure.

"We don't need another pitcher," he said aloud.

His teammates turned and looked at him.

The entire team had gathered in the dining room, after the dinner hours were over. The hotel had agreed that the Bulls could use the room for team meetings, which is what they were doing right now.

"Who says?" DeWitt shrugged. "You can never have too much pitching."

"But this is silly," Cosner said. "The man's an amateur, and you're going to let him pitch tomorrow?"

"Relax, Keith," said Sam Malone. "He can pitch in my place, not yours."

"And maybe he can replace you," Cosner said, "but not me, Malone."

"Nobody said anything about being replaced," Doug DeWitt said. "We're just giving the cowboy a look-see, that's all. Hell, he's so old he'll probably pull a muscle after one pitch."

"Then why let him pitch?" Cosner asked.

"Come on, Keith," Malone said, "don't tell me you're afraid of being shown up by an amateur."

"I ain't afraid of nothing, Malone," Cosner said. "I've been in the National League, remember? I know what it's all about."

"We know, Keith," Malone said, rolling his eyes. "You've told us the story of your professional career before."

"We know it by heart," said George Cool, and some of the others laughed.

"All right," Cosner said, standing up angrily, "play your little games if you want, but remember one thing, DeWitt."

"What?"

Cosner grinned tightly and said, "Your old amateur has to hit against me tomorrow."

Cosner turned and stalked out of the room.

"You think he'll bean Clint, Sam?" Johnny Day asked.

"He might try," Malone said. "I'm betting that Clint is a natural all the way. Pitching, fielding, *and* hitting. He'll do okay."

"Anybody else got an objection?"

"Hell, no!" George Cool shouted. "But maybe you can get the Gunsmith to put on a shooting exhibition before the game."

"Why before the game, Cool?" someone asked.

"Because if Cosner hits him in the head with the ball," Cool said, grinning, "he ain't gonna be in any shape to do anything *after* the game."

Everyone laughed, and the meeting broke up. Doug DeWitt stayed in the room, and both Sam Malone and Johnny Day lagged behind.

"What do you think, Skip?" Malone asked. "Is Cosner gonna throw at Clint?"

"He's mean enough," DeWitt said. He looked at Malone.

"Maybe it would be a good idea to give Clint an idea of what's coming, huh?"

"I'll talk to him, Doug," Malone said, "but I think he's gonna do fine."

"I hope so," DeWitt said. "For your sake."

"Why my sake?"

"Son," DeWitt said, "I've seen men killed by a baseball."

As DeWitt left Sam Malone thought, Wouldn't it be ironic for the Gunsmith, after so many years of surviving attempts on his life, to be killed by a baseball?

NINE

Clint was lying on the bed in his hotel room when there was a knock on the door. He opened the door and admitted Sam Malone, who was brandishing a bottle of whiskey.

"You didn't stay to have a drink with us, so I brought the drink to you."

"I don't have any glasses."

Malone brought his other hand around from behind his back and showed Clint two shot glasses.

"Well, don't just stand there," Clint said. "Pour."

Malone poured two glasses full and handed Clint one of them.

"What really brought you here tonight?" Clint asked.

"We just had a team meeting downstairs," Malone said.

"I thought I heard a ruckus down there."

"Yeah, well, the ruckus was all Keith Cosner."

"What's his problem?"

"You are."

"I've never even met the man."

"That doesn't matter," Malone said. "Just the fact that we're trying you out as a pitcher is enough for him to dislike you. If you were playing any other position there would be no problem."

"He can't really think I'm a danger to him," Clint said.

"Why not? I think you are."

"Sam, I threw a ball a couple of times."

"You *pitched* it, and with accuracy and velocity the likes of which I've never seen before."

"That still doesn't make me a ballplayer."

"What happens tomorrow will decide that."

"As far as I'm concerned, what happens tomorrow comes under the heading of fun. That's something I haven't had much of lately, and that's the only reason I agreed to do this."

"Well, I feel it's only fair to warn you."

"About what?"

"Keith Cosner," Malone said. "You'll be pitching in my place tomorrow, which means you'll be batting against him."

"Batting?"

"That's right. As part of the game, you'll have to hit."

"I've never even held a bat. How am I going to hit against a professional pitcher?"

"Well, I'm no great hitter, but I can show you how it's done. I think you have natural ability, Clint."

"I think you're overestimating me, Sam," Clint said. "Maybe I should reconsider this."

"No, no," Malone said. "As a pitcher, you wouldn't even be expected to hit, but you will have to stand in there against Keith."

"Well, how hard would that be?"

"Uh, well, he has indicated that he might come a little close with a pitch."

"How close?"

"He might try to hit you with it."

Clint walked over to the bed and picked up a baseball Malone had given him earlier.

"It's pretty hard," Clint said. "Feels like it could do some damage."

"There are cases of men being killed by a baseball to the head, Clint."

"I doubt that your friend Cosner would go that far," Clint said.

"I don't think so, either," Malone said, "but that doesn't mean he won't try to hit you somewhere else. Just be alert, Clint."

"I've dodged so many bullets over the years, Sam, I don't think I'll have any trouble dodging a ball."

"Let me go and get a bat and we'll go over the fundamentals of hitting."

"All right."

"After that we'll work on your fielding."

"Fielding?"

"Sure," Malone said. "You'll have to know what to do if the ball is hit back at you."

"I get the feeling that if that happens, it will come back at me a lot faster than I threw it."

"Don't worry about it, Clint," Malone said. "To tell you the truth, I don't think anyone will be able to hit off of you."

As Malone left, Clint thought that sounded a little optimistic to him. Malone appeared to be planning to make Clint into a baseball player overnight.

After a few hours of instruction, Clint suggested that he and Malone go over to the saloon for a beer.

"I'm afraid we can't do that, Clint."

"Why not?"

"Well, we have a game tomorrow," Malone said. "It's almost eleven, and I have to get to bed. DeWitt might be checking up on us any minute."

"Well, I'm not one of his players," Clint said. "Not yet, anyway. I'm going for a beer before I turn in."

"Just make sure you get enough rest, Clint," Malone said. "We're playing at ten."

"Ten? Why so early?"

"Oh, didn't I tell you?" Malone asked. "We're playing two games—one in the morning and one in the afternoon."

"When was that decided?"

"At the team meeting tonight," Malone said. "Doug said he wanted to make sure everyone got to play before we head back to Iowa."

"Well, maybe I'll play in the afternoon."

"If you do well in the morning, you can play again in the afternoon."

"Why should I play twice?"

"You want to make sure you like playing before you come to Iowa with us, don't you? I'll see you in the morning."

As Malone went out the door, Clint said, "What? Who said anything about going to Iowa, Sam?" He opened the door and stepped out into the hall. "Hey, Sam . . ."

"We'll talk about it tomorrow," Malone said, and he ducked into his room.

Clint stared down the hall for a few seconds more, then shook his head, closed his door, and headed for the saloon.

Over a beer at a back table, Clint thought about Malone's last words. The ballplayer had another thing coming if he thought Clint was going to Iowa to play baseball. Although Clint wasn't quite sure where he was headed next, he knew one thing: it wasn't to Cedar Rapids, Iowa, with a bunch of baseball players.

Clint was finishing his beer when he saw three men watching him from the bar. He knew the look and he decided to hell with the beer. He wanted to get out of the saloon before the three got brave. As he stood up, he saw that he was too late.

They were coming toward him.

TEN

Clint stood his ground and waited. From the look of these three they weren't just townspeople who had gotten all liquored up. Their guns were well worn from use, as if they made their living with them. Their clothes were travel worn, and each needed a shave. They appeared to have arrived in town within the hour and had probably gotten the word that the Gunsmith was in town.

That was the way it usually worked.

"Clint Adams?" one of them asked. He was standing in the middle.

"That's right."

They were all of a kind: mid to late thirties, the man in the center taller than the two flanking him. It was clear that he was the leader. The other two would watch him, waiting for him to make the first move. That would make them a split second slower than him, which meant Clint could take him first and then concentrate on the other two.

If it came to that. They wouldn't be as easy to talk down as the six men had been before.

"We heard you was in town."

43

"So?"

"You got a big reputation."

"I don't need you to tell me that," Clint said. "If you've got something to say, say it. If you think you've got something you have to do, then get it done. I'm busy."

"Big talker, huh?" the man asked.

"I'm not talking, friend," Clint said, "you are. In fact, I'm leaving now, so make a decision or get out of my way."

Clint saw the man's eyes flicker for a moment. It was as if he wanted to look at his two partners, only they were looking to him. The man in the center seemed to realize that what would happen within the next five seconds was entirely up to him.

"Come on, come on," Clint said. "I'm tired and I want to go to bed."

They were hardcases, these three, but they weren't dumb. The Gunsmith seemed to them more concerned about getting to bed than he was about them. That kind of disregard can take a lot out of a man.

"Hank . . ." one of the other two said.

"What?"

"Maybe this ain't the time."

Now the seed of doubt had been planted, and Clint watched it spread from face to face.

Abruptly, he kicked his chair away, startling the three men.

"Good night, gentlemen," he said, and he walked past them.

"Another time," the man in the middle called, as if trying to save face at the last minute.

Clint just waved a hand behind him and walked out of the saloon.

On his way to the hotel, he wondered how many such incidents he had been through in his life—and how many of them had gone that last fatal step.

Compared to the prospect of going through another one, playing baseball in Cedar Rapids, Iowa, didn't sound so bad.

ELEVEN

Sam Malone woke Clint early the next morning and presented him with an extra uniform of his. Then Clint loaded into the wagons with the rest of the players to ride out to the field. Most of the players were supportive of him, and although he didn't meet Keith Cosner, the man was pointed out to him. Cosner seemed to be deliberately looking away from him.

When they arrived at the field they saw that areas had been roped off for spectators.

"The people should be arriving shortly," Doug DeWitt said. "Let's give them a good show."

The manager came over to Clint and asked, "How are you doing?"

"I'm pretty nervous."

"That's natural," DeWitt said. "Uh, there's something I have to ask you."

"What's that?"

"Do you—I mean, are you . . . ah hell, aren't you gonna take off your gun when you pitch?"

Clint looked down at his holstered pistol. He knew it

must have looked out of place with the baseball uniform, but he'd had enough run-ins in this town that he didn't feel comfortable about taking it off.

"I'm afraid not."

DeWitt shrugged and said, "Just asking."

"You don't think it will intimidate the men I'm pitching against, do you?"

"Well, they're not used to hitting against an armed man. I guess we'll see, won't we?"

Clint sought out Malone and told him that he thought he had an unfair advantage now.

"What do you mean?"

"I can't take off my gun, Sam."

"I'll talk to the boys and explain," Malone said. "I'll tell them that you won't shoot them on their way to first if they happen to get a hit off of you."

"All right."

"I don't think you have anything to worry about."

"I don't know," Clint said. "I'm not anxious for that first ball to come back at me."

"That's easy to fix," Malone said.

"How?"

"Don't let them hit it."

People were starting to arrive and the ballplayers were throwing a few balls around. Clint was using Sam Malone's glove, since Malone wouldn't be needing it.

Johnny Day came up to him and said, "Let's throw some on the side and see if you've got the same pop."

Clint wondered if it weren't just a fluke the day before. Maybe today he wouldn't even be able to reach Johnny Day's glove.

That wasn't the case, though. He threw a couple of balls, and each landed in Day's glove with a resounding pop. Clint looked around and caught Keith Cosner looking at him, studying him. He looked like a man who was sizing up the enemy.

"Don't worry about him," Day said.

"You're not catching him today?"

"Doug wants me to catch you. George Cool will be catching Keith."

"I guess he's not happy about that, either."

"No, but then there's not much that Keith is happy about. Look, you'll be pitching first. We'll be going out there in about ten minutes, so get yourself ready."

"I'm as ready as I'll ever be."

When DeWitt gave the sign, one of the umpires shouted for the men to get on the field and play ball, and Clint walked to the pitcher's position.

"Come on, Clint, throw a couple," Johnny Day called.

Day crouched down behind the plate, and Clint's first pitch sailed over his head. The second one bounced about ten feet in front of the plate.

Day came trotting out to hand Clint the ball.

"Look, all you gotta do is concentrate. Block out all the people, block out everyone but the man you're pitching to— no, block out everything but me and my glove. Put the ball in my glove, Clint, and they won't be able to touch you. Got it?"

"I've got it."

"Then let's play ball."

Day trotted back to his position, and the first man came to the plate. Clint only knew a handful of the players by name, and he only knew the batter by sight. He was one of the men he'd met in the saloon yesterday.

"Okay, Clint," the batter yelled. "Let's see what you got."

Clint peered in at Johnny Day's glove and held the ball behind his back. Malone had tried to show him the pitching motion the night before, as well as the batting stance. He'd felt awkward with both, and he decided not to concentrate too much on the motion, but on throwing—or pitching—the ball.

His arm came down for the first pitch, and it whizzed by the batter before the man could get his bat off his shoulder. Clint saw the batter look down at Johnny Day, who showed him the ball.

Day tossed the ball back to Clint. He tried to catch it with the glove, but it bounced off and landed on the ground. The crowd got into him a little bit, but when his second pitch whipped by the batter into Day's glove, they quieted down.

Clint struck out all three of the batters he faced in the first inning, and none of them ever touched the ball with their bat.

By the third inning Clint had nine strikeouts, having struck out every batter he'd faced. Clint knew that he had three chances to get a batter out. If he missed the plate four times, the batter got a walk—a free trip to first base. So far, though, he hadn't missed the plate once.

Keith Cosner was keeping pace with Clint pretty well. He had given up no hits and had struck out five of the six men he'd faced.

Now, in the bottom of the third inning, Clint would be the third batter.

The first two batters made out, one of them hitting a ground ball and the other striking out.

As Clint was getting ready to walk up to the plate Malone said, "Watch him closely, Clint."

"Thanks."

Clint stepped up to the plate and swung the bat a few times. It felt awkward in his hands, and it didn't help that he had his gun on his hip. He saw the catcher looking at the gun and grinned, but he said nothing.

He peered out at Cosner and watched him carefully. He held the bat back and waited.

The first pitch came at him chest high and inside. He stepped back and the ball missed him. He felt that it had been a halfhearted effort at best, if Cosner were trying to hit him. More likely the man had simply been sending him a message.

Clint pulled the bat back into position and moved even closer to the plate.

Clint knew that Cosner was throwing fast, but the ball seemed to be coming at him slowly. Clint sometimes had the same experience when he was facing a man with a gun. There were times that he could follow every move, second by second, as if everything were happening in slow motion.

That's how the ball came in over the plate, and Clint swung.

He felt the impact up to his elbows and heard the crack of the bat—not that the bat cracked, but that was the sound it made when it made contact with the ball.

His swing had been level, something that Malone had tried to teach him in one night. The ball reversed direction and went straight back at Keith Cosner. To his credit, Cosner moved quickly to get out of the way, but he ended up on his rear end, which made the crowd laugh.

The ball went by the second baseman into center field, something Clint saw as he ran to first base. The center fielder picked up the ball and threw it back to the infield quickly, and Clint stayed on first base.

Keith Cosner had gotten to his feet and brushed himself off, and now he was staring murderously at Clint, but Clint didn't notice. He had something else on his mind.

He and Malone had not gone over what he was supposed to do if he ever got to first base.

TWELVE

"You were great," Sam Malone said.

It was late afternoon, and both games had already been played. As it turned out, Clint had not played in the second game. There had been no need. He had pitched five innings of the first game and struck out all fifteen of the batters he'd faced. He had batted against Cosner twice, getting one hit and striking out once.

"Yeah, I was great," Clint said, "except for getting—what was it Cosner did to me after I got the hit?"

"He picked you off—but that could happen to anyone."

Clint had been standing not even a foot from the first-base bag when Cosner suddenly wheeled and threw to first, picking him off.

"Small consolation for Keith," Malone said. "You really dumped him on his ass."

"It wasn't intentional."

"He'll think it was, for sure."

Johnny Day came back to the table with three more beers.

"I've never seen anything like it," Day said, shaking his head. "Fifteen strikeouts in five innings, and only three swinging strikes. Incredible."

"Beginner's luck," Clint said, but he felt particularly pleased with his performance. If he were ten years younger, he might have thought about hanging up his gun and playing baseball in the East.

"Clint, I'm sure Doug is gonna ask you to come east with us."

"You've got to say yes," Johnny Day said.

"I don't know . . ."

"What else have you got to do?" Malone asked. "Stay here and get shot at? Come with us. You'll have fun."

"And I'll help the Bulls get accepted into the National League?"

"Sure, that's part of it," Malone said. "I'd be lying if I said it wasn't. With you, me, and Keith pitching, we'll be a cinch to impress the National League officials."

"Don't forget my hitting," Johnny Day said.

"Who could forget that?"

Day had hit three home runs in the two games, one of them off of Cosner, and one off of Malone.

"I know what you guys are gonna throw before you throw it," Day said.

"We'll see how you do in the National League," Malone said.

"DeWitt probably won't even ask me."

"Oh, he'll ask you, all right," Malone said. "Doug's trying not to show it, but he's excited about you."

"He just wishes I was a little younger, huh?"

"Let's look at this realistically," Malone said. "All Doug would want out of you is part of one season. Hell, that's all any of us want out of you. You'll probably get bored after part of a season, but it'll be a new experience for you. When you want to leave, you leave, no hard feelings."

"You're certainly not dressing it up," Clint said. "I appreciate the honesty."

"Then what do you say?"

Clint was about to answer when Doug DeWitt entered the saloon. The room was less than half full, since it was dinner time, and the manager located Clint, Malone, and Day with no trouble and approached the table.

"I've been looking for you," DeWitt said, and it was not clear which of them he was speaking to, but they all assumed it was Clint.

"We're just having a beer before we go and get something to eat," Malone said.

DeWitt sat down and looked directly at Clint.

"You were damn impressive out there today, Clint," the manager said.

"Except for my base running."

"That doesn't matter," DeWitt said. "I'm talking about your pitching. I'd like you to come back east with us and play."

"Doug—"

"Before you answer, let me tell you something," DeWitt said. "I ain't promising you anything. Even with you helping us, we might not get into the National League. If we do get in, I don't expect you to stay for the whole season. Hell, I know you must be set in your ways—"

"I'll go."

"—and you are a little old to be starting a baseball career—"

"Doug, I'll go with you."

"—but I'd really appreciate it—"

"Doug!" Malone shouted.

"What?"

"He said he'll come."

DeWitt looked at Clint. "You'll come?"

"For a while."

"That's all we need you for, Clint," DeWitt said. "A while."

"But let me ask you something."

"Go ahead."

"Keith Cosner is important to this team getting into the National League, isn't he?"

"He's very important."

"How is he going to feel about this?"

DeWitt touched Clint's arm and said, "You let me worry about Cosner. You just do what you have to do to get loose to come east with us. Okay?" DeWitt stuck his hand out.

Clint took the man's hand and said, "Okay."

THIRTEEN

Clint had arrangements to make for his rig and team to be put up indefinitely. Since the team would be traveling to Cedar Rapids by train, he decided to take Duke with him. He wouldn't feel comfortable leaving Duke behind, not in a strange town. He could never be sure the big black gelding would be getting the proper treatment.

He sent a telegram to Rick Hartman in Labyrinth, Texas, to tell him that he was going east for a while. He didn't mention that he would be playing baseball. That could never be explained within the confines of a telegram.

With that done, he went back to his hotel. As he entered, he saw Keith Cosner coming down from the second floor. When Cosner saw him he scowled, and Clint knew that they were about to have their first words, and they would not be pleasant ones.

In the center of the lobby they came together.

"I know you for what you are, Adams," Cosner said.

55

"And what's that?"

"An opportunist," Cosner said. "Well, let me tell you something: You're not gonna get where you're going by going over me."

"I have no intentions of going over—"

"I'm the number-one pitcher on this team, Adams," Cosner said, cutting him off, "and no amateur with luck on his side is gonna change that."

"I don't want to change it.

Cosner frowned. "Just what are you after?"

"A little peace and quiet," Clint said. "And maybe a little fun."

"Well, this may be fun for you, but it's my life, and the lives of most of these guys on this team. You'd better not ruin that just because you want to have some fun."

Cosner left then, leaving Clint standing in the middle of the lobby, feeling a bit unsure about himself. What Cosner had said was true. For most of the fellows on the Bulls, baseball was their life. What right did he have to jeopardize that just so he could have a little fun?

Then again, a man like Doug DeWitt wouldn't be asking him to come along if he didn't feel that Clint could help the team.

If baseball was a way of life for anyone, it was Doug DeWitt, and he certainly wouldn't do anything to jeopardize it.

Clint decided to put more credence into Doug DeWitt's feelings than in Keith Cosner's.

Before meeting Clint Adams in the lobby, Keith Cosner had been in Doug DeWitt's room.

"Are you trying to sabotage this team?" he demanded of the manager.

"Sabotage? What the hell are you talking about? I want this team to get into the National League more than any of you."

"Well, you're not showing it," Cosner said. "I heard you asked that old gunfighter to come back to Iowa with us."

"That's right."

"Are you crazy?"

"You saw what he did out there today."

"A fluke!"

"A fluke? He struck out fifteen of fifteen men. You call that a fluke?"

"He's an amateur, Doug."

"So are all of the players on this team, Keith—except you," DeWitt added quickly.

"And I want to be a professional again."

"Look, Keith," DeWitt said, "I'm the manager of the team, and I make the decisions."

"Well, we'll see what the owner of the team says when we get back to Cedar Rapids."

After Cosner stormed out of the room, DeWitt thought about Clifton Davies, the man whose money kept the team afloat. It was Davies who paid for their equipment and uniforms, and it was Davies who was paying for this trip through the West.

Keith Cosner was Davies's favorite player. More than that, Keith Cosner was Davies's daughter's favorite player. Keith had been warming Olivia Davies's bed ever since he'd joined the Cedar Rapids Bulls.

Doug had often wondered which way Davies would go if it ever came down to him or Cosner.

It looked like he was going to find out as soon as they got home.

As Keith Cosner left the hotel, he was certain that when they got back to Cedar Rapids, Iowa, not only would Doug

DeWitt not be manager of the team anymore, but Clint Adams would never get to throw one pitch.

He wondered if Clifton Davies would agree to make him player-manager of the Bulls.

FOURTEEN

Clint had dinner with Sam Malone and Johnny Day.

"We'll be leaving in the morning," Malone said. "We'll catch the train in Abilene."

"I'll be ready."

"I heard DeWitt and Cosner going at it in DeWitt's room earlier," Day said.

"What did they say?"

"Keith accused Doug of trying to sabotage the team by asking Clint to come along."

"And what did Doug say?"

"That he was the manager and he made the decisions. You know what good ol' Keith said to that, don't you?"

"He's going to talk to Davies."

"Or Davies's daughter."

"Who's Davies?"

"Clifton Davies funds the team," Malone said. "He loves baseball, and he has always wanted to own a team. He's the money behind us, and if we get into the league, then he'll become our owner, lock, stock, and all."

"And his daughter?"

"Olivia," Malone said. "Every player on this team has his eye on Olivia, but it's Keith Cosner she takes into her bed—or so it's said in the society columns."

"She's twenty," Day said, "and beautiful."

"And spoiled," Malone added.

"So Cosner will go to Davies, and then what?"

"And then we'll see who Davies will support—Keith or Doug," Malone said.

"And if it's Keith?"

"Most likely Doug will be out as manager."

"Can Davies do that if he doesn't really own the team?" Clint asked.

"If he cuts off his funds there *is* no team," Johnny Day said.

"Before that could happen, Doug would quit the team," Malone said. "He'd rather quit than hurt the team."

"Maybe it's not such a good idea for me to go then—"

"Forget that," Malone said. "You made up your mind, so stick to it. It was going to come down to Keith or Doug sooner or later. I'm kind of interested in how it comes out—especially after Davies sees you pitch."

"That's it!" said Johnny Day, grabbing Malone's forearm. "We've got to make sure Davies sees Clint pitch before Keith gets to him."

"Do you really think that'll make a difference?" Clint asked.

"Don't you see?" Malone said. "If Davies sees you as the team's way into the league, that's all he'll care about. He'll tell his daughter to find herself a new ballplayer to play with."

"More than anything else, Davies wants a National League team," Malone said. "If he thinks you can get it for him, then you'll become his new favorite player."

"Why hasn't he gotten a team before now?"

"The other owners want to keep him out," Malone explained. "That's why he doesn't own the Bulls outright. Officially, we're an independent team. Once we get into the league we'll sign papers with Davies, and he can rub the other owners' noses in it."

"It sounds like it isn't all just fun," Clint said.

"Don't get discouraged," Malone said. "When you're on the field and involved in a game, everything else fades away."

"I hope so," Clint said, "because when this stops being fun—"

"We'll do our best to keep you having fun, Clint," Sam Malone said. "Once we get back home, nobody knows how to have fun in Cedar Rapids like Johnny and me."

For some reason that statement managed to give Clint more second thoughts than anything else.

FIFTEEN

Clifton Davies read the telegram again. He was reading it when his daughter, Olivia, came into the dining room to join him for dinner.

Davies was a tall, white-haired man of sixty who had taken the small fortune left to him by his father and turned it into a large fortune. If he wasn't Cedar Rapid's most prominent citizen, you would have had trouble naming someone else who was.

Olivia Davies was the toast of Cedar Rapids society. At twenty she was tall, full-breasted, and breathtakingly beautiful.

"What are you reading, Father?" she asked. She bent to kiss him and then took her seat adjacent to him.

"It's a telegram from Doug DeWitt."

"Oh. Does he say anything about Keith?"

Her father gave her a pitying look.

"Why would he? By God, girl, when are you going to learn that no one likes that strutting ass but you?"

"I thought you liked him."

"I like what he can do for the team," Davies said. "And I tolerate him for your benefit."

"Well, never mind," she said. "Keith doesn't care who likes him or not. What does the telegram say?"

"They'll be back here tomorrow," Davies said. "And DeWitt says he has a new player."

"A new player?"

"Yes, a pitcher," Davies said. "Where the hell did he find a pitcher in the West?"

"You don't need another pitcher," Oliver said. "You have Keith."

"In spite of how you feel about him, my dear," Davies said, "no team can exist with just one pitcher. You can never have enough pitching."

"Now you sound like Doug DeWitt. Really, Father, I think Keith would make a much better manager than Doug DeWitt."

"That just goes to show how much women know about baseball," Davies said. "The players will go through hell for DeWitt. They wouldn't lift a finger for Keith Cosner."

"They're all jealous of him."

"I doubt that," Davies said. "Within a year Sam Malone will be pitching rings around Keith Cosner."

"Nonsense."

"He's also a fine young man," Davies went on. "Not an arrogant or conceited bone in his body."

"Keith isn't arrogant or conceited," Olivia argued. "He's just confident."

"*Over*confident is more like it."

"Oh, Father."

"Elsa!" Clifton Davies called.

Elsa Miceli entered the room, carrying a tray of food. Elsa was in her early forties, a handsome, fulsome woman who some said saw to Clifton Davies's *every* need. She had been working for him for over fifteen years, ostensibly as his housekeeper and cook.

"Elsa, tell me who you think is a better person," Davies said as Elsa served dinner, "Keith Cosner or Sam Malone."

"I'm sure I wouldn't want to comment, sir," Elsa said. "No matter what I say, one of you will disagree." She spoke with a slight Italian accent, even though she had been in this country for twenty years.

"Good for you, Elsa," Olivia said, applauding.

"Women," said Clifton Davies, shaking his head. "They will take any opportunity to band against men."

"And why shouldn't we?" Olivia said. "If we don't help each other, who will? Right, Elsa?"

"Whatever you say, ma'am," Elsa said, and she left the room.

"I hate it when she's subservient," Olivia said.

"Only when it suits her."

"Did you have a fight with her again?" Olivia asked accusingly.

"Not a fight," Davies said. "We had a discussion."

"All your discussions turn into fights, Father," Olivia reminded him. "I think you should marry Elsa before she quits."

"I think you should mind your own business, young lady," Davies said. "Eat your dinner."

"Yes, Papa."

"Don't give me that 'Papa' nonsense," Davies said. "You're not a little girl anymore. You cannot melt my heart with a 'Papa' and a sad look. Not anymore."

"Yes, Papa," Olivia said, looking sad.

Davies cleared his throat and cut into his meat, avoiding his daughter's sad eyes. They melted his heart like butter every time, leading him to spoil her rotten. By backing the Cedar Rapids Bulls, he had effectively bought her her very own baseball player—Keith Cosner. Davies couldn't stand Cosner, but he recognized his importance to the team, and to his daughter.

"Father?"

"Yes?"

"What time will the team be arriving?"

"Nine o'clock tomorrow morning."

"Do you plan to meet the train?"

"Of course not," Davies said. "I'll wait right here for Doug DeWitt to come and see me."

"Well then, I'll meet them at the station."

"That should be a treat for all of them, my dear."

"You old flatterer . . ."

SIXTEEN

Cedar Rapids was a city of nearly eighteen thousand people, with running water, electric lights, and more than one railroad. It also had a baseball stadium, in anticipation of the day when the Bulls were a full-fledged team.

"It looks impressive," Clint said to Malone.

"It is, especially when the stands are filled with people."

As they pulled into the station, the ballplayers stood up and began to stretch. Spending the night in a railroad seat is something less than comfortable, especially if you're used to sleeping in a bed. In that respect, Clint had the advantage over his younger teammates. He had slept as often on the ground in his life as he had in a bed.

"Clint!"

Clint turned and saw Doug DeWitt bearing down on him. He had in tow the coach, Ted Banner.

"What is it, Doug?"

"I have to go and see Davies," DeWitt said. "Ted will see you to a hotel."

"He doesn't have to stay in a hotel," Sam Malone said. "He can stay with me and my mother, on the farm."

"Your mother won't mind?" Clint asked.

"Not if Doug doesn't."

DeWitt shrugged and said, "Not if Clint doesn't."

"I'd probably be more at home on a farm than I would at a city hotel," Clint said. "I accept, Sam."

"Good."

"Let's get going, then," DeWitt said. "I want to get this over with."

"He doesn't like going to see Davies," Malone confided to Clint as they made their way down the aisle to the exit door.

"If he doesn't like the man, why—"

"Because nobody else would back us," Malone said, heading Clint off. "We used to be a pretty sorry team."

"And then what happened?"

"And then Doug DeWitt took over the team and taught us fundamentals," Malone said. "He taught us what we needed to know to become winners."

"Sounds like you think a lot of him."

"I do," Malone said. "And so do most of the others— except Keith."

"What does Davies think of him?"

"Davies doesn't think much of anyone below his own station—and when you're as rich as he is, that's almost everyone."

As they stepped out onto the platform, Clint noticed that many of the players were being greeted by friends and family.

"Is your mother here?" he asked of Malone.

"No. We'll see her when we get out to the farm."

"Keith!"

Both Malone and Clint turned at the sound of the voice and saw a beautiful young woman, lavishly dressed, waving at Keith Cosner.

"Olivia Davies?" Clint asked.

"In the flesh."

"And such lovely flesh, too."

"We weren't exaggerating, were we?"

"Not at all."

As Day and Malone had told him, Olivia Davies was breathtaking.

Clint watched as the girl embraced Keith Cosner, and he wondered what such a beautiful girl could see in an arrogant cuss like Cosner.

As they walked off together, Clint looked at Sam Malone and saw for just a moment the look of pain on the man's face. Malone noticed him looking at him then, and the look disappeared, replaced by a smile.

"Ready to go?" Malone asked.

"I've got to get Duke off the livestock car," Clint said.

"I have a buggy nearby," Malone said. "I'll meet you in front of the station."

"All right."

As Malone went his way, Clint began walking the length of the train. It was clear to him that if Malone wasn't in love with Olivia Davies, he wasn't far off. Clint couldn't imagine a woman preferring a man like Keith Cosner to Sam Malone.

Malone went out in front of the station and watched as Keith Cosner and Olivia Davies got into a buggy together. There was a time when Malone thought that he and Olivia . . . But that was before Keith Cosner. As far as Malone was concerned, Cosner was no better looking, but he had once been a professional baseball player. That was the only difference Malone could see between himself and Cosner—that and the man's arrogance.

Could that be it? Could Olivia be attracted to that part of Keith Cosner?

Malone could only hope that what she felt for Cosner was infatuation, and that it would pass.

Maybe then he'd have a chance.

Clint walked Duke around to the front where Malone was waiting with his buggy. Malone looked pensive until he noticed Clint approaching.

"You want to ride him there?" Malone asked.

"I'll just tie him to the rear of the buggy and ride along with you—if you don't mind, that is."

"Nah, I don't mind," Malone said. "Climb on up."

Clint secured Duke's reins to the back of the buggy and climbed into the seat with Malone.

"Is your mother a good cook?"

"The best."

"Somehow I knew she would be."

SEVENTEEN

"He's how old?" Clifton Davies asked.

"Now, Mr. Davies—"

"DeWitt, have you gone mad?"

"Mr. Davies, if you'll just come out and see him pitch, I'm sure you'd understand what I've done."

Davies and DeWitt were in Davies's study in his house, and DeWitt had just told Davies who the new pitcher was.

"My God, man, you bring a gunman back with you and tell me he's going to be the Bulls' new pitcher?"

"He struck out fifteen men in five innings."

"I don't care—he did what?"

"Fifteen."

"That's . . . that's everyone he faced."

"That's right."

"Who did you play?"

"We split into two squads and played each other."

Davies's eyes narrowed and he asked, "Who did he strike out?"

"Among others, George Cool, Ory Sather, Jerry Cole—"

"Cole and Sather are good prospects."

"That's right, they are," DeWitt said. "Mr. Davies, if you could just get us a game with the Red Stockings—"

"I have."

"What?" DeWitt asked. "What? You got us a game?"

"Well, not a game, exactly."

"What do you mean?"

"Well, the other owners feel that anyone can win one game," Davies explained. "They want us to play a three-game series with the Red Stockings."

"And?"

"And if we beat them twice, we'll be allowed into the league."

"And if we only beat them once?"

"Then no deal."

"You didn't negotiate this yourself, did you?"

"Of course not," said Davies. "They still don't know that I'm the one funding the Bulls. I have Aaron Edwards acting for me."

Edwards was a Cedar Rapids attorney who had a good reputation. Normally, Davies wouldn't use him, but they needed his squeaky-clean front. Davies offered him a lot of money, and Edwards no doubt saw this as his entry as a high-society attorney.

"Three games," DeWitt said.

"We can pitch Cosner, Malone, and come back with Cosner again."

"Are we playing on consecutive days?" DeWitt asked.

"Yes."

"Then Cosner can't come back after one day's rest."

"Of course he can."

"No," DeWitt said, becoming excited, "we'll use Clint Adams."

"Are we back to that again?" Davies demanded. "Use one of the other pitchers."

"They're not good enough," DeWitt said. "Not for a game this important."

"DeWitt, this is madness—"

"Just come out and see him pitch, Mr. Davies," DeWitt said. "That's all I ask."

Davies stared at DeWitt across the wide expanse of his oak desk.

"If I don't like him he's off the team, right?"

"Absolutely," DeWitt said, hating himself. He had brought Clint all this way, and it was unfair to do this to him. Still, if he pitched the way he had the other day there wouldn't be a problem.

"All right," Davies said, "all right. I'll watch him pitch."

"When is this series?"

"Next Monday."

"Today is Tuesday," DeWitt said. "We have six days to get ready. We'll have a practice tomorrow, and you can see for yourself."

"This had better not be a waste of time, Doug," Davies said.

"It won't, sir, I guarantee you."

"All right, then," Davies said. "Tomorrow at the ball-park."

"Ten A.M.," DeWitt said.

Normally, he would have given the team the day off, since they had only arrived that day, but he wanted Clint accepted as soon as possible.

As DeWitt was turning to leave, he remembered something important.

"There is one other thing, sir."

"And what's that?"

"Keith Cosner."

"What about him."

"He doesn't like the idea of Clint Adams pitching for the Bulls. He, uh, doesn't like him."

"He doesn't like anyone on the team," Davies said. "What else is new?"

"No, I mean he really, intensely dislikes Adams."

"Why?"

DeWitt described what had happened when Clint and Cosner had faced each other. Davies laughed uproariously when DeWitt got to the part about the line drive that had dumped Cosner on his rear.

"I wish I had been there to see that!" Davies said. "I like this Adams already."

"Cosner could be a problem."

"If this man can pitch as you say," Davies said, "I'll take care of Cosner. Don't you worry."

"All right, sir," DeWitt said. "Thank you."

"DeWitt."

"Sir?"

"Was my daughter at the station to meet the team?"

"Yes, sir. Uh, hasn't she returned yet?"

"No," Davies said, "not yet."

"I'm sure they'll be here shortly."

"I'll see you in the morning, at ten."

"Yes, sir."

DeWitt left, wondering what hotel Keith Cosner had taken Olivia Davies to.

Davies sat back in his chair and stared off into space. No doubt Cosner had whisked his daughter from the train station to some seamy hotel rendezvous. Davies didn't like the idea, but Olivia was a grown woman and had her own choices to make.

Davies had his choices to make, too. He would choose to suffer Cosner until such time as the Bulls were accepted into the National League.

After that, there were other choices to make. . . .

EIGHTEEN

Cosner had his hands laced behind his head and was staring down at the top of Olivia's head. She was working enthusiastically on him with her mouth, and soon he was unable to maintain his relaxed demeanor. He took his hands from behind his neck and cupped her head as she rode up and down his cock with her mouth, moaning, sucking him, until he lifted his hips off the bed and ejaculated with a loud groan. . . .

Olivia Davies had the loveliest breasts Keith Cosner had ever seen. They were round and firm, and the large nipples were pink. Her light brown hair was long enough to cover them, so that he was able to just glimpse her nipples behind a curtain of hair.

She sat at the foot of the bed that way, knowing that he liked to look at her like that.

"Why don't you like this new player?" she asked.

"Well, for one thing, he's even older than DeWitt."

"W-what?"

"That's right. DeWitt's gone mad. I'm sure he's telling

your father all about Adams now."

"Do you want to talk to Father about it?"

"I don't think I have to, Olivia," Cosner said, once again lacing his fingers behind his head. "When he hears DeWitt talking about it he'll kick Doug right out of his house."

"And he'll make you manager," Olivia said, putting her hands on Cosner's legs.

"Maybe," Cosner said. "But the important thing is that we get into the league."

"That's all been arranged," Olivia said.

"What?"

She told Cosner about the three-game series Davies had agreed to through Aaron Edwards.

"Three games?" Cosner asked.

"Is that a problem?"

"We don't have a third pitcher to do the job if it goes three games," Cosner said. "I mean, I'll pitch the first game and we'll win, but Malone will pitch the second. He might lose."

"Then who would pitch the third? You?"

"Oh, sure, if I want to ruin my arm again. No, no, I'm not pitching another game on one day's rest. DeWitt would never ask me to do that."

"But you said DeWitt won't be manager anymore."

"DeWitt is a persuasive sonofabitch," Cosner said. "He might get your father to come out and see Adams pitch."

"So what? Father won't be impressed, will he?"

"Who knows?" Cosner said. "Who knows what could happen?"

Cosner got up off the bed.

"What's wrong?" she asked.

"We have to go," he said, pulling on his pants.

"But I thought we'd—"

"Your father will be worried."

"He knows I'm with you."

"Olivia, will you get dressed . . . please?"

She got off the bed and did as he asked.

Cosner was worried. Although he'd never admit it, he knew that Sam Malone was a fine pitcher, but anything could happen. They could split the first two games, and then their chance to get into the National League would rest on the third game.

And who would pitch?

Shit, he thought, if Clint Adams was really that good . . .

No, there had to be another way.

There had to be.

NINETEEN

The Cedar House Restaurant was on First Avenue, and if you sat at the front window you could see the First Avenue bridge. The two men were not seated at a front table, however, but at a back table against the far wall. Anyone watching the two men, who were drinking coffee, might assume that they were waiting for someone, and waiting impatiently.

The assumption would be correct.

Kenneth Selma shook his head and said, "Ten more minutes and I'm either going to order lunch or leave."

Selma, like his companion, was a wealthy man and an owner of a National League team. Most of his money had been made in construction.

"We'll order," his companion said. "He'll be here. He's usually late. It gives the illusion that he's busier than we are."

The second man was Peter McBain. He was also the owner of a professional baseball team. His money was made in commodities—buying, selling, trading.

The three men met here whenever they were in town and had something to discuss. In this instance, their discussion concerned the Cedar Rapids Bulls. Of the eight National League teams, five owners had voted to allow the Bulls to try to "play" their way into the league. The three dissenting votes had come from Kenneth Selma, Peter McBain, and the man they were waiting for.

The waiter came over to the table and asked, "Would you like to order now, gentlemen?"

Selma and McBain exchanged glances, and then McBain said, "Yes. Kenneth?"

"Steak."

"I will have the chicken," McBain said. "Our friend will have the salmon."

"Shall I bring it or wait until he arrives?"

"Bring it."

"But it will be cold by the time he arrives."

"That's all right," McBain said. "He likes his food cold."

The waiter nodded and went to get their orders.

"You're a mean man," Selma said.

"It's what he deserves," McBain said. "Always lording it over us, making us wait for him."

"Next time," Selma said, "we should just leave."

"Agreed," McBain said, but both men knew that was nonsense. The man they were waiting for could buy and sell both of them.

None of the three men lived in Cedar Rapids—or even in Iowa. Selma was from Illinois, and he owned the Chicago White Stockings. McBain was from New York, and he owned the New York Giants. The man they were waiting for, William Ryker, was the owner of the Cincinnati Red Stockings.

Although these three men owned the best three teams in the league, their votes carried no more weight than the other five owners'. Outvoted five to three, they had no choice but to watch the games and hope that the Red Stockings could defeat the Bulls.

Eventually the meals were served. Ryker's salmon was set before his empty seat.

"Why didn't Ryker refuse to have the Red Stockings play the Bulls?" Selma asked. "That would have solved everything."

"Then they would have asked me to let the Giants play. If I refused, they'd have asked you to let your team play. If we all refused, we'd be breaking up the league. We don't want that."

"And we don't want an inferior team allowed in."

"If they're inferior," McBain said, "the Red Stockings will prove it."

"*If?* You have doubts? One of their pitchers is Keith Cosner. Only an inferior team would need a retread like him—a troublemaker."

"Maybe."

"Peter, don't tell me you want the Bulls in the league."

"Only if they deserve to be in the league," McBain said. "If they beat the Red Stockings—"

"If they beat them, Ryker is going to be very embarrassed."

McBain laughed. "It would bring him down a peg or two, wouldn't it?"

Both men laughed together, but they stopped as the door to the restaurant opened, admitting William Ryker.

"Ah, you've ordered," Ryker said, seating himself.

"Yes," McBain said, "it was getting late."

"Yes," Ryker agreed, looking down at his salmon. It was what he usually ordered.

"What have you found out?" Selma asked.

"I've checked on the attorney, Aaron Edwards, but I wasn't able to find out who he represents."

"Then we still can't prove that Davies owns the Bulls," Selma said.

"No," Ryker said, picking up his utensils.

"But who else in Cedar Rapids could?" McBain asked.

"No one," Ryker said, "but we can't prove it. Not yet."

"Once they're in the league," McBain said, "he could buy the team, and there's nothing we could do about it."

"Correct."

"Then we have to make sure that the Bulls don't beat the Red Stockings."

"Right," Ryker said.

"And how do we do that?" Selma asked.

"If several of their best players were injured," Ryker said, "that would do it."

McBain and Selma exchanged glances, and McBain said, "That would do it, all right."

Ryker cut into his salmon and lifted a piece to his mouth.

"Hey," he complained, "this salmon is cold."

TWENTY

Lunch at the Malone farm was more than Clint could have hoped for. Then again, given the surprise he'd already received, nothing should surprise him anymore.

During the ride from the train station to the farm, Clint had decided to broach the subject of Malone and Olivia Davies.

"I get the feeling," he said, "that you are more than just an admirer of Olivia Davies."

Malone looked at Clint for a moment, probably trying to decide whether to lie or not.

"It shows, huh?"

"It shows, kid."

"I thought I had a chance for a while," Malone said, "but then Keith came along, and that was the end of that. He's all she can see."

"Well," Clint said, rather lamely, "maybe it will pass."

"That's what I'm hoping."

"Tell me about your farm. Does anyone live there besides your parents?"

"My mother lives there alone when I'm not around,"

Malone said. "My father died ten years ago."

"I'm sorry."

"We'll be a little late for breakfast," Malone said, "but wait until you sample one of my mother's lunches."

"I'm looking forward to it."

"Of course, first we'll have to do some chores."

"Chores?"

"My mother always said that no one eats until they do their chores."

"Your mother sounds like a wise old woman."

Clint did not notice the smirk that formed on Malone's mouth at that point.

"There it is," Malone said some time later.

Clint saw the house, and the barn, and a small corral with two horses in it. Beyond the house there was a pasture with some cows in it. As they approached the house, he saw the chickens alongside the house and the chicken coop directly behind it.

"It's not much," Malone said, "but it feeds Ma and me."

"I guess that's all you could want."

Malone stopped the buggy right in front of the house and said, "I'll look inside and see if Ma's there. You can look around."

"Why don't I take the buggy and Duke over to the barn?"

"Okay, sure."

They got down, and while Malone went into the house, Clint walked the buggy and Duke over to the barn, with intentions of making them comfortable. As he entered, he saw something that brought him up short.

There was a woman in there, and she was bent over with her back to him. He found himself looking at as fine an ass as he had ever seen, clad in denim. Clint cleared his throat, and the woman straightened and turned.

It was clear that she was no young girl—probably in her early forties—but the front was at least as fine looking as the rear. She had a pair of proud, high, firm breasts and fine long legs. Her hair was black, with some gray streaked into it, and worn short. Her eyes, wide set, were brown, and her mouth was wide, with full lips. At the moment she was frowning, her head cocked to one side.

"I didn't mean to frighten you."

"You didn't."

"Or startle you."

"You didn't."

"Well . . ." Clint said. "I didn't know anyone would be here. Sam—uh, Sam Malone—told me his mother lived here alone."

"She does."

"Well, then, I didn't know anyone worked for her."

"No one does."

"Well then," Clint said, becoming exasperated, "I'm a little bit confused."

"So am I," she said. "Who are you?" When she asked the question, she was looking directly at the gun on his hip.

"My name is Clint Adams," he said. "I'm a friend of Sam Malone's. And you are . . ."

"Dee Malone."

"Malone?" Clint repeated. "Now I'm really confused. Sam didn't say anything about having a sister."

"He doesn't."

"Then that means that you're—"

"Oh, I see you found her," Malone said, entering behind Clint.

He walked past Clint to the woman, kissed her on the cheek, and said, "Hello, Mother."

He turned and grinned maddeningly at Clint, who was somewhat stunned.

"She's really something, isn't she?"

Clint found his voice and said, "That makes two of you."

After Sam and Dee Malone laughed at the joke, she left Malone and Clint in the barn to go and prepare an early lunch.

Malone unhitched his horse while Clint unsaddled Duke. They got both horses fed and rubbed down and started back for the house.

"Do you think she'll have any other chores to do?" Clint asked.

"No," Malone said, "I think she'll feed us before she really puts us to work."

"I'll bet you and your mother thought that was funny," Clint said.

Malone laughed. "It was my joke," he said. "She didn't know anything about it."

"Well, she certainly didn't fess up right away, did she."

"My mother is a woman of few words," Malone said. He laughed again. "When you referred to her as a 'wise old woman' I knew you'd be surprised when you finally saw her."

Malone was right. All along Clint had been picturing a white-haired old woman of sixty or so. Dee Malone could not have been more than forty-eight, and she could have been as young as forty. Clint decided to settle on a comfortable, very attractive forty-five.

"I was surprised, all right," Clint said. "But pleasantly so."

"Got your eye on my mother already, huh?" Malone said, slapping Clint on the back.

"I'll let you know," Clint said. "After I taste her cooking."

TWENTY-ONE

Lunch was a feast.

There was chicken Dee had prepared because she knew Sam would be coming home that day. She had also prepared fresh corn bread that morning, and she had made a pot of strong, black coffee.

They all sat around a heavy wooden table and fell to eating while Malone told his mother about the trip to the West. Dee Malone listened attentively, but from time to time she'd glance at Clint, who would only smile.

"It all sounds very exciting," Dee said to her son. "How did you come to hook up with my son, Clint?"

"That's the best part of the story, Ma," Malone said, and he then proceeded to tell about his meeting with Clint.

She listened with great attention to the story of the discovery of Clint's pitching prowess.

"This is all very interesting," Dee said. She looked at Clint and asked, "And you never knew you had this . . . this talent?"

"I never had any reason to discover it, Mrs. Malone," Clint said. "My 'talent,' as you call it, has always been for hitting what I shoot at."

"I see."

"The same talent applies itself to baseball, Ma," Malone said. "He can throw the ball right where he wants it. It's incredible. And the speed!"

"I'm impressed."

"Don't be."

"You'll be even more impressed when you hear about his reputation."

"Sam . . ."

"They call him the Gunsmith!"

"Sam!"

Malone stopped talking, then grinned sheepishly and said to his mother, "He's modest."

"Modesty doesn't enter into it," Clint said. "Some things just aren't worth bragging about."

"I think I understand," Dee said.

"Thank you."

"I *don't* understand," Sam Malone said.

"That's because you're young," his mother said, reaching over to caress his face.

"Aw, Ma . . ." he said, batting her hand away.

"Are you finished with your lunch?" Dee asked her son.

"All done."

"Good," she said. "The cows broke through a length of fence near the south fork. I was waiting for you to come home and fix it."

"See?" Malone said to Clint. "Chores. Come on, Clint, you can—"

"Clint is going to stay here and have some more coffee with me, Sam," Dee Malone said. "We're going to get acquainted. You go and fix that fence. You've done it before."

"Well, all right," Malone said. "I'll be back in a few hours. You watch she don't give you something to do, too, Clint."

"Sam," Dee said, scolding her son, "Clint is our guest."

"Yeah," Malone said with a smile, "but you'll put him to work anyway, soon enough. I know you will."

"You get out of here."

"I'm going," Malone said, and he went out the door.

Dee Malone stood up, grabbed the coffeepot from the stove, and asked Clint, "Another cup?"

Clint held his cup out. "Yes, please."

Clint and Dee spent the next hour getting better acquainted. She explained what it was like trying to raise a son and run a farm alone after her husband had died.

"Sam was a big help once he grew big enough," she said. "It really hasn't been all that difficult since he got some size to him."

Clint tried to explain to her why he had come all this way to try and play baseball at his age.

"I'm not all that sure of the reasons, myself. I guess I was just ready for something new."

"And?"

"And . . . I suppose I figured no one would be shooting at me here. Nobody would be wanting to try me."

"Well, if they don't know who you are . . ."

"I don't brag about it, Mrs. Malone."

"Please, call me Dee."

"All right, Dee."

"I'll talk to Sam," Dee said. "I can see that he's excited about having you here. I'll try and make him understand the importance of not bragging about your . . . reputation."

"I'd appreciate that, Dee," Clint said. "He's a good kid."

"I know," she said. "I just wish he'd forget about this baseball thing."

"It will be hard on you here if he goes off to play ball, won't it?"

"I just don't think anything is going to come of it."

"Well, if the team doesn't make it into the National League, nothing will, and then he'll be around all the time."

"I know he doesn't want to be a farmer all his life, but . . . well, it was good enough for his father and me, do you know what I mean?"

"I know."

"So you're going to help them get into the National League, huh?"

"I doubt it," Clint said. "I really don't know what I can do."

"Well, someone must feel you can do something. After all, you are here."

"Yes, I am," Clint said. "And while I'm here I expect to earn my keep. Tell me what I can do."

"No, no," she said, "you're a guest."

"If you don't let me work, I'll have to go stay in a hotel in town, and that will be expensive."

She paused a moment and then said, "Yes, yes, I suppose it would be. Well, the chicken coop could use some mending."

"Where can I find some tools?"

"In the barn."

He stood up and said, "I'll get right on it. After that you'll have something else for me to do?"

"I will," she said. "I promise."

"All right."

"I'll also have a big dinner waiting for both of you when the work is done."

"I'll look forward to that," Clint said.

Clint went out the door, and Dee Malone sat at the table, staring after him. There was one thing she hadn't told him about: the loneliness she had felt during the past ten years.

Maybe a man like Clint Adams would be the answer to that—at least for a while.

TWENTY-TWO

The lunch at the Cedar House Restaurant was winding down.

William Ryker was the last to finish, because he had ordered a fresh salmon dinner, one that was hot. Selma and McBain had started on coffee and cake before Ryker was done with his salmon.

"Well?" McBain said.

"Well what?" Ryker asked.

"How are we going to do this?"

Ryker looked at McBain and Selma and said, "I'll take care of it."

"How?"

"I'll take care of it."

"Wait a minute," Selma said, suddenly wary. "Nobody is going to get hurt, are they?"

"I thought that was the point," Ryker said. "A few key players get injured, and the Red Stockings won't have any problem at all beating the Bulls."

"I think what he means is that nobody is going to get

killed, are they?" McBain asked.

"Killed?" Ryker said, pushing his plate away. "Why would anyone get killed?"

"Just so you know," McBain said, "we won't go along with any killing."

"Don't worry," Ryker said. "Just leave it to me. Peter, you know the Bulls roster. Who are the key players on the team?"

"Well, there's Cosner, of course."

"That retread?"

"He gives them the experience, and he can still pitch," McBain said. "He's number one."

"All right," Ryker said. "Who's next?"

"The kid pitcher, Sam Malone," McBain said. "After that there's the catcher, Johnny Day. He's their best hitter."

"Any more?"

"One other," McBain said, "a prospect named Jerry Cole. He's the shortstop, and he's got the best hands I've ever seen."

"All right," Ryker said. "Where do they all live?"

"Cosner, Day, and Cole live in town. Malone lives on a farm about five miles north of town."

"All right," Ryker said. "I'll put some men on it."

"No killing, remember?" McBain said.

"Peter," Ryker said, "I'm a banker, not a killer. Remember?"

"Sure, William," McBain said. "Sure, I remember."

Selma and McBain exchanged unsure glances. They both knew of incidents in which Ryker had had someone killed to get what he wanted.

"Where is that waiter?" Ryker asked. "I'm ready for my dessert."

After lunch Peter McBain, Kenneth Selma, and William Ryker each went their separate ways.

Ryker went to his hotel and up to his suite. In a room adjoining his suite was a man named David Drake. Ryker walked to the connecting door and knocked, then took off his jacket and tie.

The connecting door opened and David Drake entered. He was tucking his white shirt into his pants. Beyond him, before the door closed, Ryker caught a glimpse of a naked woman on his bed.

"You wanted me, sir?"

"Yes, David, sit down."

David Drake was a tall, well-built man in his early thirties. He was officially a vice-president of one of William Ryker's New York banks, but to Ryker he was something else. He was his troubleshooter.

"I'll try not to keep you too long," Ryker said to Drake.

"That's just something to pass the time, sir," Drake assured him.

"Nevertheless . . . David, we have a small problem."

"The Bulls, sir?"

"Precisely."

"Are they owned by Davies?"

"We haven't been able to establish that, but there is a way we can be sure that the Bulls won't make it into the league."

Drake laughed and said, "The Bulls can't beat the Red Stockings, sir."

"Maybe not, but there is a way for us to make sure."

"How is that, sir?"

"I'll need you to round up some men who won't be afraid to do some . . . dirty work."

"What kind of dirty work?"

"Does it matter?"

"Yes, sir," Drake said. "On any street corner I can find you a man who will hurt someone or break a bone for money. If you want someone killed—well, that's more money, and I'd have to look elsewhere. Which do you want?"

Ryker took a moment to think it over before responding to the question.

"Why don't you find us a few men who will do *anything* for money. That way we'll have all our bases covered."

"Yes, sir."

"All our bases . . ." Ryker repeated. "I believe that's pretty funny, Drake."

"Yes, sir," Drake said, "it is. Shall I get on this right away?"

Ryker looked beyond Drake to the connecting door and said, "Uh, you might want to finish what you're doing first."

"I'd prefer to get right to it, sir."

"All right then, Drake," Ryker said. "Why don't you just send the young lady in here then. Uh, just so she won't be too disappointed, that is."

"Yes, sir," Drake said. "Thank you for taking her off my hands."

"My dear Drake," Ryker said, "friends do for each other."

Drake entered his own room and looked at the woman reclining on the bed. Her name was Rachel. She was a tall, leggy brunette with small but nicely rounded breasts. He had seen her on the street in front of the hotel and approached her right then and there. When she'd asked him why he had approached her he'd said, "Because you look like you'd do anything for money."

Instead of becoming insulted and slapping his face, she had said, "You're right."

"Who was that?" she asked now.

"He is my boss, sweetheart," David Drake said, approaching the bed and picking up her clothes along the way, "and you're going to go in there and show him a good time, aren't you?"

She reclined on the bed on her back with one leg bent and her hands flat on her stomach. "And why should I?"

"Because, darling," he said, helping her into a seated position while handing her her clothes, and, speaking in hushed tones, he said, "He has even more money than I do."

She smiled lasciviously. "That's a very good reason."

He showed her to the connecting door and she stopped just short of opening it.

"But what about us?"

"Darling," he said, kissing her neck, "we will have all night."

"Well, all right," she said. "What's his name?"

"His name is Mr. Ryker," Drake said. "If he wants you to know more than that, he'll tell you."

Drake opened the door and ushered her through, patting her on the bottom and blowing her a kiss.

When she was gone he collected his shoes, tie, shoulder-holstered .38, and jacket, and he went out to do his job.

That was the way he thought about his gun: just another piece of his apparel.

David Drake was the only "bank vice-president" who walked around New York City armed.

TWENTY-THREE

Sam Malone was quiet at dinner.

There was something in the air that he could feel but could not identify.

The kitchen was a separate room from the dining area, so when his mother got up to go into the kitchen to get something, Malone leaned over to Clint.

"Did something happen between you and my mother this afternoon?"

"What do you mean?"

"I mean . . . did you have an argument or something? Did she get mad at you for any reason?"

"I don't think so," Clint said. Something had happened between them, something unspoken, but there was no way he could explain that to Sam Malone—even if the woman involved were not his mother.

"Well, I'll have to talk to her," Malone said. "She's been very quiet during dinner."

"You've been quiet during dinner," Clint said. "In fact, it's been a nice quiet dinner. There's nothing wrong with that, Sam."

"No, no," Malone said, "my mother usually talks a lot during dinner. She's got something on her mind."

"Did it ever occur to you that it might be her business?"

Malone started to reply, but his mother came back at that moment, so he sat back in his chair.

"What are you two talking about?" she asked.

"Nothing," Sam Malone said quickly. He said it in such a tone that Clint knew this young man had never been deceitful in his life.

"It was nothing," Clint said, shaking his head so that she would not pursue it.

They finished their dinner, and Dee Malone was clearing the table when she heard the horses outside.

"Sam, would you go out and see what's bothering the horses? In fact, why don't you put them in the barn."

"All right, Ma."

After Malone had left, Dee turned to Clint and asked, "What was going on?"

"Sam thought he . . . detected something in the air."

"Like what?"

"Something between us, I suppose."

"Like what?" she asked again.

"He thought you were angry with me."

"Well, I'm not."

"I told him that."

"What else did you tell him?"

"That maybe you had something on your mind that was your business."

"What do you think?"

"About what?"

"Was there something in the air between us?"

He stood up. "What do you think, Dee?"

He moved around the table toward her, but before he could reach her they both heard a shot from outside.

"Stay inside!" he said, grabbing his gun from a peg on the wall on the way out.

When Sam Malone left the house he headed for the corral, but he was still thinking about his mother. As he approached the corral he noticed that the horses were skittish. That usually meant that there was a coyote or— worse—a wolf in the area.

"Easy, boys," he said to them. "Take it easy."

"That's good advice, son," a voice said.

He turned quickly, but not quickly enough. A fist struck him in the stomach, doubling him over. A second man came from the other side and grabbed him by the hair.

"If you're a smart boy," the second man said, "you'll take your beating like a man."

"What—"

"Uh-uh," the first man said, "no questions. Just pain. Haul him up onto his feet."

As the second man leaned over to grab him, Malone came up quickly, striking the man beneath the chin with his head. The man grunted, and Malone pushed the first man out of his way and started to run toward the house.

The second man, his tongue cut by his own teeth, angrily pulled his gun.

"No, don't!" the first man said. "There's not supposed to be any—"

But the second man was blinded by the taste of his own blood, and in anger he fired.

Clint came out the door as the man fired a second shot. The bullet hit the wall near his head. He saw Malone running toward him, and beyond him, framed in the moonlight, he saw the shooter setting up for a third shot. He'd missed his first two, but they couldn't count on him missing his third.

"Get down, Sam!" Clint shouted. "Hit the ground and roll!"

Malone heard Clint's words and obeyed them. He hit the dirt and went into a roll, kicking up dust. Clint raised his gun and fired before the shooter could squeeze his trigger a third time. Clint's bullet struck home. He watched the man stagger and fall, and he thought he saw a second man but couldn't be sure. Still, he advanced cautiously, his gun ready, moving toward the fallen man until he was crouched over him.

He turned the man over and checked for a pulse, but he was already dead. He turned and saw Sam Malone coming toward him, with Dee hurrying up behind.

"Sam, are you all right?" she asked, grabbing her son's arm.

"I'm fine, Ma," he said. "Thanks to Clint."

"What happened, Sam?" Clint asked.

"I was checking the horses and these two men jumped me," Malone said. "They wanted me to take my beating like a man, they said."

"This one's dead," Clint said. "I'm going to check around for the other one. Do you have a gun in the house?"

"A rifle, yeah," Malone said.

"All right, go inside and wait for me."

"Clint—"

"Take your mother back to the house, Sam, and make sure that rifle is loaded. Don't come out until I come back."

"Clint—" It was Dee Malone this time.

"Let's go, Ma," Malone said. "Let's do what Clint says."

"Be careful," Dee said as her son pulled her toward the house.

TWENTY-FOUR

Clint did a thorough search of the grounds around the house and barn. He checked inside the barn and even inside the newly repaired chicken coop. Satisfied that the second man was not around, he stuck his gun into his belt and dragged the dead man into the light given off by one of the windows of the house.

"Sam?" he called.

The door opened and Malone stepped out, carrying an old Henry rifle.

"You can come out."

Malone came close and Dee Malone stepped out of the house.

"Do you know this man, Sam?"

Sam Malone came closer and studied the face of the dead man. Clint's bullet had caught him in the throat, leaving the face untouched.

"I don't know him, Clint," Malone said, shaking his head.

"Dee?"

Dee Malone moved closer so she could see the man's face more clearly.

"I've never seen him before."

Clint looked at Malone and asked, "Then why were he and his friend going to give you a beating?"

"They didn't say."

"Did they say anything?"

"Just that I should take my beating like a man. Then one of them told the other to haul me to my feet. I came up under his chin with my head."

Clint leaned over and pried the dead man's mouth open.

"He's got a cut tongue. This is the one you hit with your head. You made him mad enough to shoot at you."

"Wait a minute!" Malone said. "I did hear the other man say something else."

"What?"

"He was telling this one not to shoot, that they weren't supposed to kill anyone."

"All right," Clint said. "At least that tells us something."

"What?" Dee asked.

"They were sent here to give Malone a beating, maybe even to hurt him, but not to kill him."

"Why would they want to beat him up?"

"Maybe they wanted to hurt him enough so that he couldn't play baseball."

"What?" she asked.

"Why would they want to do that?" Malone asked.

"I don't know, Sam, but it's all I can come up with. We haven't been back long enough for you to get somebody mad at you, so unless they were settling an old score . . ."

"There is no old score."

"Then come up with a better explanation."

"Why would someone want to keep me from playing ball?"

"Maybe somebody doesn't want the Bulls to make it into the National League."

"Why single Sam out?"

"He's one of the better players on the team," Clint said.

"They think that hurting me is going to stop the Bulls?"

"Maybe," Clint said, "you're not the only one they're after."

Jerry Cole was coming out of his hotel when two men suddenly grabbed him. They each hit Cole in the stomach, and then one told the other, "Hold his arm out."

While one held Cole's arm straight out, the other came down on the arm with his elbow. The sound of his bone breaking was like a crack of thunder to Jerry Cole, and the pain caused him to pass out.

"Leave him," said the man who'd broken the arm, and the other man released him.

Both men walked away, leaving Jerry Cole lying on the ground.

Johnny Day was coming out of the rooming house where he stayed when two men tried to jump him. Day heard their feet scraping the ground and turned in time to avoid the first blow, meant for his head. He moved away, then grabbed the man's arm as it went by and pulled. The man came stumbling toward him, and Day hit him with his left hand on the point of the jaw. The man fell to the ground, stunned, and the second man tripped over him.

Johnny Day turned and ran faster than he had ever run from home plate to first base.

Two men waited outside the hotel where Keith Cosner had a room, but Cosner never showed up. After a few hours they gave up, meaning to try again the next day.

● ● ●

"Let's put the body out behind the barn until we can go for the law in the morning," Clint said to Malone. "Grab his feet."

Malone handed the rifle to his mother and grabbed the dead man's feet.

"Go on inside now, Dee," Clint said. "It's all over for tonight."

Dee Malone went inside while Clint and Sam Malone carried the dead man and dumped him behind the barn.

"I noticed a buckboard in the barn," Clint said. "In the morning we'll take him into town and turn him over to the law."

"We'll have to talk to Doug and the others then," Malone said, "and warn them."

"If my guess is right," Clint said, "and someone is trying to hurt your team's chances, then I'd say that they'll try for the three or four best players on the team. Who would those be?"

"Me, I guess," Malone said, "Keith Cosner, Johnny Day . . ."

"And after that?"

"I guess that'd be up to whoever's picking," Malone said. "Could be George Cool, or Jerry Cole, or any of a half-dozen other players. Then again," Malone added, "it could be you."

"I don't think anyone in Cedar Rapids knows yet that I'm on the team."

"Clifton Davies knows by now."

"He wouldn't try to hurt his own team," Clint said. "Besides, I don't think anyone would try for me until they saw what I could do."

"We have a practice at ten tomorrow morning," Malone said. "We'll have to get an early start if we're going to turn this body in."

"We can warn the others at the practice." Clint slapped Malone on the back and said, "Let's get some sleep."

"You don't think they'll try again tonight?" Malone asked, obviously nervous. "I'm not afraid, mind you, but I worry about Ma."

"One of their men got killed," Clint said. "They'll reexamine the situation before they try again."

Malone bowed to Clint's superior knowledge in this kind of situation.

As they were walking back to the house, Clint didn't tell Malone what he was thinking. It made sense that whoever was behind this would set it up to happen all on the same night.

At practice tomorrow they'd find out who else had been attacked tonight and who might not have been as lucky as Sam Malone.

TWENTY-FIVE

The next morning Clint and Sam Malone went out and loaded the body onto the buckboard. Riding into town in it would not be as comfortable as it might have been in the buggy, but they had to get the body to the proper authorities and then get on to practice. Malone was anxious to warn his teammates about the danger. Clint was even more anxious to find out if any of the others had already been attacked the night before.

Dee Malone came out of the house while they were preparing to leave.

"You have nothing to worry about, Dee," Clint said, trying to assure her. "They were obviously out to hurt Sam, not you."

"I'm afraid that doesn't make me feel any better, Clint."

"I'm sorry," Clint said. "I only meant that you were safe enough. No one will try to hurt you."

"I have the rifle in the house, Clint," she said, "and I know how to use it. Just keep your eye on Sam, will you, please?"

"Of course I will."

"And save an eye for yourself, too."

"We'll be fine, Mother," Malone said. "I don't think anyone will be foolish enough to come after me again. Not after what happened last night."

"I hope not."

"We'll be back for dinner," Malone shouted as they drove away.

William Ryker got out of bed and stretched. The session he'd had the night before with the girl had been . . . diverting, but he had dismissed her soon after. He could not sleep with anyone else in bed with him.

He prepared himself for breakfast, which he had arranged to have brought to his room at eight o'clock each morning. Drake would be joining him. They usually went over the previous day's business at breakfast.

He wondered how last night's business had gone.

Drake was worried, and even the fact that Rachel's talented mouth was riding up and down his penis couldn't chase away his worries.

He had to figure out how to tell William Ryker that not only had last night's maneuvers failed, but that one of their men had been killed as well.

Only one player out of the targeted four had been disabled, and Ryker wasn't going to like that. Ryker had not told Drake how much time they had. Drake could only hope that it didn't all have to be done by today.

Rachel moaned as she felt Drake's penis swelling, and Drake lifted his hips and momentarily forgot everything else as her mouth sucked him dry.

"Ah, there you are," Ryker said as Drake entered through the connecting door. "Breakfast has only just arrived."

Breakfast had been served on a table with wheels, and Drake sat down opposite Ryker with little enthusiasm for food.

"What's wrong?" Ryker asked. "Are you going to ruin my breakfast?"

"I'm afraid so."

Ryker, a good fifty pounds overweight and proud of it, frowned.

"Very well," he said then. "Before I start eating, go ahead."

Slowly, Drake told Ryker everything that had happened last night. He started with the fact that young Jerry Cole now had a broken arm, then moved on to the fact that Johnny Day had gotten away, followed that with the fact that Keith Cosner had not been found, and then finally explained what had happened at the Malone farm.

"Malone killed a man?" Ryker asked.

"No, not Malone," Drake said. "Apparently there was another man there, and he killed one of the men I hired. The other man got away."

"Why was there any gunfire at all?"

Drake had no good answer for that.

"Somebody lost his head—panicked, I guess."

"We can't afford that," Ryker said softly—more softly than Drake might have expected. He expected the full force of Ryker's famous temper. Maybe Ryker was mellowing in his old age.

Drake poured coffee for both of them as he considered the situation.

"The Bulls will be playing the Red Stockings on Monday," Ryker said. "You have until then to make sure that they can't win. I want to know who that was at the Malone farm last night. I want to know who they have that is willing to kill for them."

"Yes, sir."

"I want to know *that* as soon as possible, Drake," Ryker said, his voice growing colder at that moment. "Do you understand?"

"Uh, yes, sir, I understand," Drake said. "I'll take care of it."

Ryker removed the cover from the tray of breakfast, beaming at the eggs, bacon, biscuits, and potatoes. Drake looked down at the food with absolutely no craving whatsoever.

"I'll get right on it, Mr. Ryker," Drake said, getting to his feet. "If that's all right with you."

"Fine, Drake," Ryker said, filling his plate. "That's just fine."

Drake stood up to leave, and Ryker said, "Oh . . . Drake."

"Yes, sir?"

"That young lady that was here last night?"

"Rachel?"

"Yes, that's the one."

"What about her?"

"Could you have her here again tonight?" Ryker asked. "Just for a while, mind you. Not the entire night."

"Yes, sir," David Drake said, "I'll take care of that, too."

TWENTY-SIX

Malone drove the buckboard to the police station, an imposing, two-story brick structure. They left the body in the back, climbed the stairs, and entered.

There was a large wooden front desk that reminded Clint of police stations in St. Louis and New York. The policeman behind it could also have been from either of those places.

"Excuse me," Clint said. "but we have a body we'd like to give you."

The man's jaw dropped.

Inspector Roger Gunn made Clint and Malone tell their stories again. The body had been removed from the buckboard half an hour before, and they still had practice to get to, which would start in about ten minutes.

Malone told his part, and then Clint told his part. The inspector said, "I think we should go over this again."

"All right," Malone said, but Clint cut him off.

"I don't," Clint said. "I think we've gone over this enough."

"Do you?" Gunn asked.

"Yes, I do," Clint said. "We defended ourselves, brought you the body, and told you the story. Now we have other things to do."

"You haven't told me why these men would want to administer a beating to Mr. Malone."

"If I knew that," Clint said, "I *would* have told you, Inspector."

"Would you?"

"Sure," Clint said, "why wouldn't I?"

"I don't know, why wouldn't you?" Gunn asked. "Look, Adams, I know who you are."

"You do?"

"I know you have a big reputation in the West," Gunn said. He stood up, a man six-four who looked six-eight because of his ramrod-straight back. Also, he had a way of looking down his nose at you that made it seem as if he were looking at you from an even greater height.

He came around the desk and stood in front of Clint, who was seated. Clint did not look up at him. He would not give the man that satisfaction.

"This is not the Wild West, Mr. Gunsmith," Gunn said. "We don't go around shooting people."

Clint stood up and looked Gunn in the eye.

"You do when they're shooting at you," he said. He looked at Malone. "Come on, Sam. We have a practice to go to."

Clint and Malone were the last to arrive at practice, something that did not escape the attention of Doug DeWitt.

"It's damn well about time," DeWitt said.

"We have to talk," Clint said.

"I have a practice—"

"It's important, Skip," Malone said.

The practice was being held in an open field, not at the baseball stadium. The stadium would be saved for the actual games.

"All right," DeWitt said. "Ted! Take them through their paces one more time."

"Without those two?" Banner called back.

"Yeah," DeWitt said, "without these two." He looked at Clint and Malone. "Well."

"Somebody tried to hurt Sam last night," Clint said.

DeWitt frowned. "What do you mean, someone tried to hurt him? How?"

Clint explained what had happened, and DeWitt listened in awe—or shock.

When Clint had finished, DeWitt said, "Somebody broke Jerry Cole's arm last night."

"Oh, Jesus," Malone said.

"How'd it happen?" Clint asked.

"Two guys jumped him. Cole says they deliberately broke his arm."

"Let's find out if anyone else had any incidents last night."

"We don't have to do that," DeWitt said. "Two guys jumped Johnny Day, but he got away from them."

"Three incidents," Clint said. "What does that tell you, Doug?"

Instead of answering the question, DeWitt said, "I talked to Clifton Davies yesterday. We have three games with the Cincinnati Red Stockings."

"Three games?" Malone asked excitedly. Then he frowned and asked, "Why three games?"

"If we win two of them, we're in the National League," DeWitt explained.

They all stood quietly for a moment, watching the rest of the team exercise.

"Obviously," Clint said, "somebody doesn't want us to win."

"But who?" Malone asked.

"I don't think that matters," DeWitt said. "What matters is that we *do* win two of those games, no matter what."

"All we have to do is keep the team in one piece between now and Monday," Clint said. He looked at DeWitt and said, "We have to warn them."

"After practice, Clint," DeWitt said. "We'll tell them after practice."

"Why after?"

"Davies is gonna watch us work out today," DeWitt said. "That's why we're out in the middle of nowhere."

"So?"

"I don't want them to have anything on their minds but the game."

Clint hesitated and then said, "That's reasonable, but before they leave here I want everyone to know."

"Agreed. Now, one more thing."

"What's that?"

"You're pitching," DeWitt said. He looked at Clint anxiously. "You can pitch today, can't you?"

"Sure I can. Why not?"

"I don't know. I just wanted to make sure."

At that moment a fancy buggy pulled up at the far end of the field and stopped. No one got out.

"He's here," DeWitt said.

"Doug," Clint asked, "am I on display?"

"You damn well are, Clint," DeWitt said. "We all are."

TWENTY-SEVEN

They split into two squads and played a game. DeWitt pitched Clint and Sam Malone against each other. He didn't want to use Cosner, because he didn't want any incidents. Naturally, Cosner was angry enough to spit, which he did almost every time Clint walked out to his position.

He also did a lot of muttering, but *loud* muttering, so that DeWitt would be sure to hear him.

"Who the hell does he think he is? . . ."

"He expects to get into the National League this way? . . ."

"He's so senile he's using senile pitchers. . . ."

"Wait until Clifton Davies hears about this. . . ."

"Keith," DeWitt finally said, "if you've got something to say to Davies, walk out there to his buggy. Otherwise, shut up."

That shut Cosner up because he hadn't know that Davies was in the buggy. He wondered if Olivia were out there with him.

He watched the rest of the game glumly as Clint struck out fifteen of the eighteen batters he faced. DeWitt took him out after six innings, and put in another pitcher to finish the game.

"Why won't you let me pitch, Skip?" Cosner finally asked. His tone was very close to being a whine.

"Keith, damm it," DeWitt said, "You've got nothing to prove."

"Not to you, maybe . . ." Keith muttered, this time under his breath.

Clint watched the rest of the game standing next to Doug DeWitt, who talked incessantly about the fundamentals of the game. Clint listened intently, surprised at how much went into the game of baseball. The first time he ever saw the game it was hit the ball, catch the ball, throw the ball. He had never suspected how much more there was to the game.

It didn't matter who won—even though the squad Clint was playing on won, one to nothing—and after the game DeWitt gathered all the players together.

First, he told them the news about the three-game series with the Red Stockings.

"Settle down!" he shouted as they whooped and hollered. "This team is not going to be easy to beat, you know."

"Don't worry, Doug," George Cool said, "we'll beat 'em."

"We have to beat them twice," DeWitt pointed out. "I don't want anyone thinking this is gonna be a walk in the park, understand?"

Everyone indicated, by word or nod or shrug, that they understood.

"All right. We have another practice tomorrow at eleven, right here. Everybody be here."

"Everybody's not here today," someone shouted.

"What happened to Cole?" another player shouted. "Prospects don't have to practice?"

"No." DeWitt said coldly, "it's hard to practice when your arm has been broken."

"What?"

DeWitt explained then what had happened to Cole, what had happened to Day—who was surprised that his wasn't an isolated incident—and then what had happened at the Malone farm. When he told them that Clint had killed one of the men, another cheer went up.

Clint waited for the noise to die down and then said, "A man being killed is nothing to cheer about."

"Yeah, but you saved Sammy's life," George Cool said.

"I wish I could have done it without killing anyone," Clint said. "Maybe if I had, we'd have been able to find out who hired the guy."

"So what's going on?" Day asked.

DeWitt deferred to Clint and allowed him to answer the question.

"My best guess, since there were three incidents, is that someone is trying to hurt the team by trying to hurt the team's best players."

Keith Cosner snorted. It was clear that he disagreed, since no one had tried to hurt him.

"I wouldn't feel insulted, Keith," Clint said. "I'd be willing to bet that if we checked around your hotel we'd find out that a couple of guys were waiting around for the better part of the night."

"Are you a detective now?"

"No," Clint said, "I'm not a detective."

Keith spit onto the ground and said, "You're not a ball-player, either," and he walked away.

The players watched Cosner walk away. Some of them still thought of him as a leader and wondered if they should follow.

"All right, eyes front," DeWitt called out. "Listen to what Clint has to say."

"From now until the games are played, I don't want anyone going out alone," Clint said. "Travel in pairs, or groups. It's very important that no one go out alone."

"Does that include me?" Ted Banner asked. "I'm not even a player, let alone one of the better players."

Everyone laughed, but Clint said. "Even you, Ted. Let's not take any chances with anyone, all right?"

"Who is it we're supposed to be afraid of?" Clyde James asked.

"Right now anyone you don't know," Clint said. "We don't know who's behind these attacks, and, as I told Keith, I'm not a detective."

"Have the police been notified?"

"I'm sure Jerry spoke to them, but I think Doug should talk to them later today."

"I'll do it," DeWitt said, "right after I talk to the man."

At the mention of "the man," Clint looked out to where Clifton Davies's buggy was, and it was still there.

"All right, that's all," DeWitt said. "Remember what we said: Don't go anywhere alone."

As the team scattered, in twos and groups, Clint turned to DeWitt and said, "I guess he's waiting to talk to you, huh?"

"Take the kid home," DeWitt said to Clint, "and keep an eye on him. I'll come out to the farm later."

"All right," Clint said, "but what about Cosner?"

"What about him?"

"He left here alone."

"I'll have a couple of the boys go to his hotel, maybe even Ted Banner."

"Why Ted?"

"Ted used to play professional ball. I think Cosner respects him, if nobody else."

"All right," Clint said. "We'll see you at the farm."

"And hey."

"What?"

"Watch out for yourself, too."

A lot of people seemed to be telling him that lately.

TWENTY-EIGHT

Clint and Malone went back to the farm, and Clint stayed with the younger man through all his chores.

As they were cleaning up for dinner, Clint said, "I've never worked on a farm before."

"It's not that bad."

"It's hard work."

They were each washing in a bucket in the barn. Malone grabbed a towel and then turned to face Clint.

"It's backbreaking work," Malone said. "It killed my father. I'm not going to let it kill me and my mother."

"Is that why you started playing baseball?"

"Sure," Malone said. "Hey, there are only two things I can do, Clint: play ball and work on a farm. You've done both now. Which would you rather do?"

"Play ball."

"That's right." He put the towel down. "Do you know that I could make as much as eight thousand dollars a year playing professional ball? I mean, that's top dollar, and I'll probably make less than that, but even half that would keep my mother from killing herself on this farm."

"Have you ever asked your mother what she thinks about working this farm?"

"What do you mean?"

"Your father started this farm, didn't he?"

"Sure . . ."

"He died working it, right?"

"Yes."

"This place is all she has left of him—this place and you. Do you think she wants to give any of that up?"

Malone looked shocked for a moment, then said, "Uh, I guess I never asked her."

"Maybe you should."

"Yeah," Malone said. "Yeah, maybe I should."

As they left the barn to walk to the house, they saw a buggy approaching. They reached the house and waited for the buggy to join them. When it was close enough, they recognized Doug DeWitt.

Dee Malone came out, drawn by the sound of the buggy, and smiled.

"It's Doug."

Clint looked at Dee, then Malone, and then at Doug DeWitt as he stepped down from the buggy. Dee stepped forward and embraced Doug. Clint wondered what was between them.

"You're just in time for dinner, Doug."

"One of your dinners, Dee? That's worth the ride out here."

"I'll take care of the buggy," Malone said.

Clint entered the house behind Dee and DeWitt, feeling somewhat out of place.

"Do you two know each other a long time?" he asked.

"We met when I discovered Sam," DeWitt said.

"Doug's been looking after Sam for me, haven't you, Doug?"

"I look after all the boys, Dee," DeWitt said, "but yeah, I guess Sammy's one of my favorites." DeWitt gave Clint a quick look and said, "Don't you let me catch you ever telling him that."

"Not me, Doug."

Malone came back into the house, having washed his hands again after seeing to Dewitt's horse and rig, and Dee started laying out dinner.

"What did Davies have to say?" Malone asked.

DeWitt looked at Clint and said, "He was impressed, Clint."

"What's that mean?" Clint asked.

"He's gonna try and keep you on the team."

"What would keep me off? Cosner?"

DeWitt shrugged. "Davies is gonna talk to Keith."

"You mean it's up to Keith whether I stay with the team or not?" Clint asked

"No, not exactly. What I think is going to happen is that Davies will explain to Keith why you should stay with the team. He'll then see how Keith will react."

"He might walk off the team," Malone said.

"He might threaten to," Clint said, "but I don't think he will."

"Why not?" Malone asked.

"He wants it too bad," Clint said. "He'll bluster and threaten, but I don't think he'll walk, and he won't take a chance that Davies will cut him loose."

"I agree," Dee said, entering the room. "That's the kind of man Keith Cosner is—all bluster and boast. He thinks every team wants him, and every woman, but he'll never take a chance that either one will decide the other way."

All three men looked up at her, and at least two of them were wondering how she knew so much about Keith Cosner.

"I agree, too," Dewitt said.

Dee set the soup tureen down with a bang.

"Keith Cosner is a horrible man. I will not have him discussed at my dinner table during dinner. Is that understood?"

All three men exchanged glances, and Clint said, "I understand it."

"So do I," DeWitt said.

Sam Malone grinned and said, "Let's eat."

TWENTY-NINE

Clint was sitting on the front porch later that night, looking out into the darkness. He hadn't told Dee or Sam Malone, but basically he was on watch.

Douglas DeWitt had left an hour before, and Malone was seeing to the stock, putting them in for the evening. Dee was still inside, cleaning up after dinner.

They still had four days to go before Monday morning, when, according to DeWitt, the first game would be played. DeWitt had named Cosner as the pitcher in the first game and Clint as the pitcher of the second game.

"Before any of you object," DeWitt had said then, holding up both hands, "Sam, I want to hold you out for the third game because you've got the experience over Clint."

"You expect Clint to lose?" Malone had asked.

"No," DeWitt remarked, "but I don't know that I expect him to win, either."

"I don't understand," Malone said.

"Neither do I," Clint said.

"That makes three of us," Dee Malone said.

121

"It's really very simple," DeWitt said. "If something happens and either Keith or Clint lose, the second and third games will be pressure games. I wouldn't want Clint's first game to be that third one. I think Sam can handle the pressure better than Clint would."

Both Sam and Dee Malone had said that they understood. Clint did not comment then. If he had, he might have made someone angry, because what he would have said was that—first, second, or third game—he didn't feel *any* pressure. His career—his *life*—was not riding on these three baseball games. He was here for a month or two at most, and then he'd be heading back to the West, where he belonged. Cosner, Malone, and the others would still be here.

Clint actually felt that he'd be the ideal pitcher for that third, pressure-packed game, because he'd be the only player in a Bulls uniform who was feeling *no* pressure whatsoever.

DeWitt was the manager, though, and it was his job to name the pitchers.

Dee came out at that moment and stood next to Clint.

"See anything?" she asked.

"No," he said, "but I'm not looking for anything."

"Sure you are," she said. "You're—what do they call it in the army?—you're on sentry duty."

Clint laughed and said, "I'm standing my watch."

"Whatever," she said. "Do you want Sam and me to stand a watch also?"

"No, that won't be necessary."

"You can't stay up all night."

"I don't intend to," Clint said. "I do intend to sleep out here, however."

"I'm sorry we have no guest room."

The previous night Clint had slept in the barn, on a bed of hay. Tonight he intended to sleep right there on the porch.

He didn't think anyone would be able to get near the house without waking him.

"Will you be comfortable?" she asked.

"No," he said, "but then that's not the idea, is it?"

"I'll get you some blankets," she said, and she went inside.

Malone came out of the barn and joined Clint on the porch. Clint told him that he would be sleeping outside.

"You miss sleeping under the stars, huh?" Malone asked, too naive to understand why Clint was really sleeping outside.

"I do, yeah," Clint said.

"Well, I'm gonna turn in. We got another workout tomorrow morning."

"Good night, Sam."

"G'night, Clint."

Malone passed his mother in the doorway. She had two blankets for Clint, one for him to spread out and lie on, and one if he got cold. April in Iowa could still scare up quite a chill.

"I'm afraid I don't really understand all of this," she said.

"All of what?"

"All of this . . . violence on behalf of a . . . a game. I mean, baseball is just a game, isn't it?"

"To some people it's a game," Clint said. "To others it's a business. It's the people who are involved in it as a business who are prone to violence."

"In other words, the people who own the teams?"

"Yes," Clint said. "Some of the owners—or one of them, at least—do not want to see the Bulls get into the National League."

"Why not?"

Clint shrugged. "Reasons of their own, I guess."

"Will we ever know?"

"We might, and we might not. I don't think we should concern ourselves with that, though."

"Why not?"

"If the Bulls win two of those games, it will all be over. They'll be in the league and there'll be nothing anyone can do about it."

"So all you intend to do is try to keep everyone safe until then?"

"That's right," he said, "and then it will be up to the team."

"Clint, what will you do if the team makes it into the league?"

"I'm not sure."

"Will you travel with them, play the other teams in the other cities?"

"I don't know yet, Dee," Clint said. "I'm still not really sure why I came along at all."

They stood there, very close together, looking out into the darkness.

"It's strange," she said.

"What is?"

"In all the years I've lived here, I've never been afraid."

"And you are now?"

She hugged herself, as if she were cold, and said, "Yes."

"Don't be," he said, putting an arm around her. "I won't let anything happen to you."

She leaned her head on his shoulder.

"And Sam?"

"Him too."

"Thank you, Clint."

He looked down at her, and she lifted her head and kissed him on the mouth.

"Good night," she said.

"Good night, Dee."

THIRTY

The night passed uneventually, as did the next two days. By Saturday morning, several people were becoming impatient.

One was Clint himself. He knew that other attempts were to come, but he didn't think they would be this long in coming. His only guess was that whoever was behind the attacks wanted to make sure he had men he could trust this time. Men who wouldn't panic under pressure.

Clifton Davies was impatient.

He wanted Monday to come, because he was afraid of attacks, but also because he wanted the games to be played. The schedule called for two games Monday and the third—if necessary—on Tuesday.

Davies wanted it all to be over by Monday night, with the Bulls finally in the National League.

Then by Tuesday morning, he would be the legal owner of a National League baseball team, and he would rub it into the faces of all the other owners.

• • •

William Ryker was perhaps the most impatient of all, along with Kenneth Selma and Peter McBain.

Over breakfast at the Cedar House Restaurant, Peter McBain said, "I thought you were going to take care of this, William."

"I am, Peter."

"Well, we've only read in the papers about one player being injured. That's not going to stop these games, you know."

"I'm aware of that."

"Then what's—"

"It's being handled."

"By who?"

"By someone I trust. He wants to make sure he has men he can trust before we try again."

"Why?"

Ryker made them wait while he chewed a mouthful of eggs and bacon.

"We've found out who the other man was at the Malone ranch."

"Who was it?" Kenneth Selma asked.

Ryker himself had received this news from Drake Thursday night, and because of it he understood and concurred with his man's decision to go slow and wait until they had enough reliable men to do the job.

"His name is Clint Adams," Ryker said. "The dime novels refer to him as the Gunsmith."

"I've seen some of those things in New York," McBain said. "In fact, some years back the man himself was in New York. The newspapers even call him the Gunsmith. I believe he was involved in solving a murder."

"Surely a character from a dime novel," Kenneth Selma started, but Ryker cut him off.

"He's much more than that," Ryker said. "It was his

exploits that inspired the dime novels. He is a true figure of the West, like Wild Bill Hickok and Buffalo Bill Cody."

"Well, what the hell is he doing in Iowa?"

"Apparently," Ryker said, "he's pitching for the Bulls."

"What!" McBain said in shock.

"That can't be!" Selma said.

"Well, it is, believe me."

"How old is this legend of the West?" McBain asked.

"Near as I can ascertain, he's over forty."

Suddenly, Peter McBain started to laugh, and the other two men stared at him.

"What the hell are you laughing at?" Selma asked.

"Don't you see it?" McBain asked. "The humor? The joke? How can the Bulls hope to win when one of their pitchers is a forty-year-old legend of the West? A gunman? It's a grand joke, don't you see?" McBain looked at Ryker and said, "Your team will run right through them in two games."

"That's very possible," Ryker said. "However, I don't think this should change our plans."

"I agree," Selma said. "Let's go ahead as planned."

"Very well," McBain said, still chuckling, "but I must tell you both that I no longer consider the Cedar Rapids Bulls a threat."

"Any team," William Ryker said, "can beat another team on any given day."

"Yes, but—"

"You of all people should know that, Peter," Ryker said. "Your Giants beat my Red Stockings one game—in the last five years."

McBain stopped laughing and frowned, and suddenly Kenneth Selma was laughing, as if he now saw the joke.

When Ryker returned to his hotel he met in his room with David Drake.

"What have you to report?" Ryker asked.

"I finally have the men I want," Drake said. "Today the Bulls will lose three of their best players."

"And Clint Adams," Ryker said.

"And Clint Adams," Drake said with assurance. "I have three good men to take care of him."

"All right," Ryker said, "then take care of him. I want him killed."

"What?"

"Killed," Ryker said again. "Dead. Do you have a problem with that?"

"I don't have a problem with it, but I don't understand it."

"It's just something one of my colleagues said this morning," Ryker said. "He said he didn't consider the Bulls a threat anymore. I concurred with that, but I'm afraid I don't feel the same about Clint Adams."

"I see."

"Can your men do it?"

"The men I have should be happy to do it," Drake said. "They know who Adams is, and it would enhance their reputations to kill him."

"Good God," Ryker said, "they won't brag about it, will they?"

"They might," Drake said, "but they won't say who they were working for when they did it."

"All right then," Ryker said, "see to it."

"Yes, sir."

Ryker lit a big Cuban cigar and walked to the window to look at the street below.

By that night, Clifton Davies would be shitting bricks, wondering what he was going to do for a National League team.

THIRTY-ONE

After practice on Saturday, Malone and Johnny Day told Clint, "Let's go and get a beer."

"I don't know . . ."

"What's the harm?" Johnny Day asked. "We'll be together."

"I'm getting stale, Clint," Malone said, "going back to the farm all the time."

Clint relented. "All right," he said. "We'll go get a beer."

"A couple of beers," Johnny Day corrected.

Clint nodded and said, "A couple of beers—but first I want a bath."

"Good idea," Malone said.

They went back to Johnny Day's place and took turns taking a bath, and then Day and Malone led Clint to a small tavern.

"Whataya think?" Day asked.

"Not bad," Clint said. The place was small, brightly lit, and half full on a Saturday afternoon. The bartender knew both Day and Malone.

"Hey, Johnny, Sammy," he said, setting three beers on the bar. "Are you fellers gonna do Cedar Rapids proud on Monday?"

"Now, how'd you hear about Monday, Chris?" Johnny Day asked.

"Hey, everybody knows about it," Chris said. "It's an important day for all of us. If the Bulls can make it into the National League, you guys could put Cedar Rapids on the map."

"We'll do the best we can."

There was an empty table in the back, and they took their beers with them and occupied it.

"So what's going on?" Day asked.

"What do you mean?" Clint asked.

"You had us all thinking somebody was gonna try and hurt us or something," Day said. "How come nothing's happened?"

"I don't know," Clint said, "but something will."

"How can you be so sure?"

"Johnny," Malone said, "Clint's been through this kind of thing before."

"Yeah," Day said, "in the West, not here."

"Look," Clint said, leaning forward, "if nothing happens, I'm all for that. I'm not looking to be proven right."

"What's the matter with you, Johnny?" Malone asked.

Day tapped his fingers on the table next to his beer and then said, "I guess I'm just tired of looking over my shoulder."

"You know what will happen the moment you stop, don't you?"

"No, I don't—but I know what you're telling me."

"What Clint is telling us is for our own good, Johnny," Malone said. "You know what happened to Jerry Cole, and you know somebody tried to do the same thing to you."

"I know, I know," Day said. "I'll just be glad when this is all over."

"All we have to do is win two games," Malone said, "and it will be."

"Yeah . . ." Day said.

Clint studied Johnny Day and wondered how many of the other players were feeling the pressure. Then again, a lot of them knew they weren't among the top three or four players on the team. The only pressure they were feeling was from the upcoming games themselves, not from looking over their shoulders.

"Another one?" Malone asked Clint.

"Yeah," Clint said, even though he still had half a beer left. "Another one."

Outside of the tavern, three men stood across the street. These three men—Stern, Sackett, and Green—were all men who had worked for David Drake before.

"Think we're the only ones covering this place?" Stern asked.

"You heard Drake," Green said. "The other men he hired aren't smart enough to warm a chair. They're just hired to break bones, not think. Sure, I think we're the only ones here. Some of the team members come here sometimes, especially on a Saturday."

"Adams has got two other players with him," Sackett said. "What do we do about them?"

"Nothing," Green said. "We were hired to take care of the Gunsmith, and that's what we're gonna do. If the other two get in the way, well, there's nothing we can do about that, right?"

"Right," Stern said.

"How are we gonna do this?" Sackett asked.

"Like I said," Green said, "we weren't hired to break bones. Besides, this is the Gunsmith—we don't take any chances. Understood?"

"Yeah," Stern said, nodding to Sackett, "we understand."

THIRTY-TWO

"How about another one?" Johnny Day asked.

"I don't think so," Clint said. "We should get back to the farm."

"Why don't we go someplace else?" Malone suggested.

"Sam . . ."

"Come on, Clint," Malone said, "it's Saturday. Let's do something."

"Normally, I'd say fine, let's do something," Clint said, "but all we'd be doing is making targets out of ourselves."

"What have we got to worry about?" Malone asked, slapping Clint on the back. "We've got the Gunsmith to protect us."

Clint slapped Malone's hand away, and the kid looked confused.

"Don't call me that," Clint said.

"I—"

"And don't be so sure that you're safe just because you're with me."

"Hey," Malone said, his eyes wide, "I'm sorry, Clint . . . I—I didn't mean—"

"Let's get out of here," Clint said, standing up. Malone stood up as well. "Johnny?"

"I'll stay."

"You're coming, Johnny," Clint said. "I'm not leaving you here alone."

Just then three or four more of the players walked in, and Johnny Day said, "I won't be alone."

"Johnny . . ." Malone said.

Johnny Day looked up at Malone and Clint, then sighed and said, "All right, all right, I'm coming."

"Remember," Green said to Stern and Sackett, "no stray shots. We're supposed to be pros, remember?"

Sackett nodded, and Stern said, "We remember."

Johnny Day walked out the door first, followed by Sam Malone. Day stepped left, Malone right, and Clint stepped out, standing between them, momentarily framed in the doorway.

"Now!" Green said, and they commenced firing.

Clint's sixth sense had warned him about trouble from across the street. Just before firing, the three men stood up, and Clint caught the movement.

"Down!" he shouted, drawing his gun and dropping into a crouch.

He heard the lead slamming into the door behind and above him. Very deliberately he fired back at the three men, aided by the fact that he didn't have to cock his double-action Colt.

One man spun away as a slug struck him in the chest, and another reflexively grabbed his face as a bullet struck him between the eyes.

The third man, seeing that his comrades were down, started running up the street.

"Stay here!" Clint shouted, and he started running after him.

The man was across the street, and at first Clint ran parallel with him on his side of the street. Finally, he decided to cross over, and as he did so a milk truck blocked his path. He stopped short and went around the truck, finding that he'd lost a good ten or fifteen feet on the fleeing man.

Ideally he wanted to take the man alive to find out who he was working for, but once the man turned and started firing at him he had no choice. He pulled the trigger twice and the man doubled over, stayed that way for a few seconds, and then fell over onto his face.

THIRTY-THREE

Clint, Malone, and Day sat at the same back table while Inspector Gunn and his men cleaned up the mess. The tavern had emptied out in the wake of the shooting, and the bartender stood behind the bar, looking glum.

"I'm gonna get a beer," Day said. "Anyone want one?"

"No," Clint said, and Malone shook his head.

Clint watched Gunn while Day went to the bar. He expected the inspector to give him a bad time for killing three men, but at least he had Malone and Day as his witnesses.

Day returned with a beer and said, "Having someone try to kill you really shakes you up."

"Nobody tried to kill you," Clint said.

"What do you mean? How can you tell—"

"Look at the pattern of bullets on the door. Not one slug went astray in either of your directions."

"Meaning what?" Day asked.

"Meaning those three were trying to kill me."

"Because you're playing on the team?"

Clint looked at both Malone and Day and said, "Unfortunately, I'm never quite sure why people try to kill me. It's usually because of my reputation."

"Do you think that's the case now, Adams?" The speaker was neither Malone nor Day, but Inspector Gunn.

The inspector sat with them at the table and said, "Well?"

"I don't know, Inspector," Clint said. "I can't be sure."

"Well, it can't be because you're one of the best players on the team, can it?"

"It might," Malone said. "If anyone had seen Clint pitch in practice they'd know how good he is."

"And who's been watching you practice?" Gunn asked.

"Nobody," Clint said.

"Nobody but Mr. Davies," Malone said, and both Day and Clint looked at him. The entire team had been sworn to secrecy about Davies's involvement. Naturally, that many people couldn't possibly keep their mouths shut for very long, but it hadn't been very wise of Malone to blurt out the name in front of Gunn.

"What's this? Clifton Davies? What's his interest in the team?"

"You'll have to ask him," Clint said. "I'm sure we don't know."

"Yeah," Gunn said, "I'm sure. Adams, I'm going to have to ask you for your gun."

"No chance."

Gunn frowned. "Our citizens don't just walk around carrying guns."

"These three did."

"They might not be citizens."

"Neither am I."

"Adams—"

"Inspector," Clint said, "you take my gun you might as well paint a target on my chest."

"I can take you in."

"Go ahead," Clint said. "I'd probably be safer in one of your cells."

"You can't take him in," Malone said. "He's got to pitch game two."

Gunn looked at Malone and said, "Not if you lose both games Monday."

"And what do you know about Monday?" Clint asked.

"Come on," Gunn said. "Everybody knows about Monday."

"You wouldn't happen to have a bet down, would you, Inspector?" Clint asked.

"Me, bet?" Gunn said, standing up. He grinned and said, "Why do you think you're *not* in a cell right now?"

"Because I fired in self-defense."

"Yes, well," Gunn said, "there is that."

Gunn turned to leave, and Clint said, "You will let me know if you get an indentification on those three?"

"After my chief," Gunn said, "you'll be the first to know."

"And who they work for?"

"Adams," Gunn said, "do me a favor."

"What?"

"Concentrate on baseball."

"I would, if people would stop shooting at me."

Johnny Day was nervous enough to accept Sam Malone's invitation to come and stay at the farm.

"I don't want to get you mad at me, Clint," Day said, "but I'd feel safer at the farm."

"I'm not mad, Johnny," Clint said, "but just remember, those three were after me, and they didn't want to just hurt me, they wanted to kill me."

"Well, the way I figure it," Day said, "the ones looking for me and Sam are still out there."

"We got to get back to the farm, Clint," Malone said anxiously. "Ma's there alone."

"I don't think she's in any danger, Sam," Clint said, "but I agree. Let's get back to the ranch."

THIRTY-FOUR

"Another failure?" William Ryker said to David Drake.

"It wasn't really our fault, sir," Drake said. "The Gunsmith was just too good for my three best men. Also, he has Malone and Day with him, and we can't get near them."

"What about Cosner?"

Drake checked his watch.

"He's probably being taken care of right now."

"For your sake, Drake," Ryker said, "I hope so."

Keith Cosner came out of his hotel and started walking up the block. He was supposed to pick up Olivia at her house. That would give him a chance to talk to Clifton Davies about what was going on with the team.

As he reached the corner and started across, three men stepped from a doorway and grabbed hold of him. Two held his arms while the other moved around in front of him. None of the three had said a word, but Cosner instinctively knew that this was what Clint Adams had been talking about.

These men were going to hurt him.

Suddenly Cosner felt panic. If he allowed this to happen, if he allowed these men to hurt him, even slightly, then his chance to get back into professional baseball would disappear. Nobody would give him another chance after this.

He couldn't allow that.

Blindly, he kicked out and caught the man in the midsection. With more strength then he would have ever thought, he possessed, he pulled away from the two men holding him and began swinging wildly. Suddenly, he realized that instead of standing and fighting he should be running, and he ran, trying to get away, waiting for a shot to ring out, waiting for a bullet to strike him in the back.

By the time the three of them got to the ranch they had agreed not to tell Dee Malone what had happened at the tavern. In spite of that, Clint could see that she knew something had happened. Sam Malone had a face incapable of guile, especially when it came to his own mother. Clint doubted that she believed their story about stopping for a beer and losing track of the time.

Dinner was a quiet affair, except for Johnny Day periodically telling Dee Malone how delicious it was. That was another giveaway that something was being kept from her in the general silence of the table.

After dinner Clint suggested to Malone and Day that they take Malone's rifle and go have a look around the grounds.

After they had left, Dee stopped cleaning the table and sat down opposite Clint.

"All right, what happened?"

"What do you mean?"

"Don't give me that, Clint Adams. Something happened today that no one is talking about, and my son looks like he's keeping a secret and is about to burst from it. What happened?"

So he told her, making sure she knew that the attempt had been on him, not on her son.

"You killed all three of them?"

"I had to."

"No, no," she said, looking at him strangely, "of course you did . . . I know you did." It was clear that the concept of one man killing three was hard to accept—or maybe it was simply the concept of killing that was alien to her.

At that moment Malone and Day came back into the house, and Malone set the rifle down in a corner.

"Not finished cleaning up yet?"

"No," Dee said, "and you can help. Johnny, sit down and have a cup of coffee with Clint."

While Malone helped Dee clean the table, Day and Clint had coffee and talked.

"What are we gonna do?" Day asked. "We just have to get through tomorrow and tomorrow night."

"I have an idea how to do that."

"How?"

"I think we should go and talk to Mr. Davies tomorrow," Clint said.

"Why him?"

"Because even though the team is not yet his officially, he might have some idea who is trying to sabotage us."

"All right," Day said, "so let's go and see him."

"See who?" Malone asked, reentering the room.

"Davies," Day said, and he explained what Clint had suggested.

"Sounds good to me," Malone said, "but maybe we should talk to DeWitt in the morning first. He'll want to go with us."

"That's fine," Clint said. "Why don't we get an early start and do just that."

Day and Malone agreed.

"In that case, I think we ought to turn in early, boys."

"This early?"

"This early."

"Where do I sleep?" Johnny Day asked, looking around.

"On the floor," Clint said. "Sam, you sleep in the same place you've been sleeping."

"My own bed . . . thanks . . . And where are you gonna sleep?"

"I'm going to sleep in the barn," Clint said. "In the hayloft."

"Why the hayloft?" Malone asked.

"I can see everything from up there," Clint said. "No one will be able to approach the house without me seeing them."

"Are you expecting someone?"

"No," Clint said, "not after what happened today, but there's no harm in being careful."

"Are you sure you don't wanna take turns?" Malone asked.

"No," Clint said, "I'll handle it. You guys get your sleep."

Dee Malone entered the room with three blankets. She gave one to Day and two to Clint.

"Sweet dreams, men," she said, and she went into her bedroom.

"I'll see you fellers in the morning," Clint said, and went to the barn with his blankets.

THIRTY-FIVE

Clint had made himself a bed of hay in the hayloft, positioned so he could look down at the house and the grounds surrounding it. He was about to lie on it when he saw someone come out of the house. It was Dee. He watched as she walked from the house to the barn. There were no lights on in the house.

"Clint?"

"Up here, Dee."

She climbed the ladder to the hayloft, and he looked at her from his bed of hay.

"You look comfortable."

"Uh, yes, it is kind of comfortable. Uh, Dee, what brings you out here?"

"Johnny and Sam went right to sleep. They were snoring so loud I couldn't sleep."

"So you came out for a little air?"

She smiled down at him and said, "I could tell you yes, I came out for some air, but that wouldn't be true."

"What is the truth, Dee?"

"You know the truth, Clint," she said. "There's been something between us ever since you got here."

He stared at her, then said, "Yes, there has, but is this the time to do something about it?"

"I've been waiting for the right time, Clint," she said, her hands going to the buttons on her shirt, "and it just hasn't come. This time I'm *making* it the right time."

She unbuttoned her shirt and peeled it off, dropping it to the floor of the hayloft. Her breasts were large and firm looking, the nipples dark and distended. The light from Clint's storm lamp made shadows on her skin as she undid her pants and leaned over to slide them down her legs. Her big breasts hung and swayed as she moved, and Clint's hands began to itch. Her legs were long, her thighs a little too heavy, but at her age she could be forgiven for that.

When she was naked, she moved toward where he was sitting. She put her hands on his shoulders and used her weight to push him down on the haybed. The length of her big body was pressed against his, and he could feel her heat right through his clothes.

She pulled his shirt free from his pants and slid it up so she could run her hands over his chest and kiss his flesh. She undid his pants and got to her knees to pull them off him. He discarded his shirt and lifted his hips so she could help him off with his underpants. When he was naked, he grabbed her and pulled her down on top of him. Her mouth came down on his and their tongues began to thrash against each other.

"God," she said against his mouth. "Oh God, I can't wait . . ."

She sat up on him, took hold of his penis, lifted her hips, and came down over him, taking him inside of her. She began to ride him up and down, coming down on him heavily and gasping each time. He reached up and cupped her breasts, squeezing them and pinching her nipples.

He rolled her over, and hay clung to their sweat-laden bodies. He reached beneath her to cup her big buttocks and began to take her in long, hard strokes. She gasped into his ear and clung to him with her arms and legs. As he drove into her, he lifted his head and saw a rider approaching the house.

"Dee . . ." he said.

"Hmm?"

He withdrew from her and she opened her eyes, having trouble focusing on him.

"Dee, someone's coming."

"Oh God!" she said, reaching for him, but he was gone, pulling his pants on and grabbing his gun.

She sat up as he began to climb down, her breathing ragged, her heart pounding.

Next time, she thought, next time . . .

Clint ran from the barn with his gun in his hand, and as he approached the house the figure began to dismount.

"Hold it!" Clint called.

The man turned quickly, his hands thrust into the air, and Clint saw that it was Keith Cosner.

"What the hell!" Clint said.

"Can I put my hands down?"

"Yeah, put 'em down."

Cosner took his hands down and put them on his butt.

"I don't know how you Westerners do it," he said. "My butt is killing me."

They were all inside, sitting at the table with fresh coffee in front of them. Dee Malone had a flushed look to her face, but nobody noticed—nobody but Clint. He could also *smell* her, and he wondered if anyone else could. Probably not. They were all probably interested in Cosner's presence, and the reason for it.

Clint could smell her, though. . . .

"So what are you doing here, Keith?" Malone asked.

"Look," Cosner said, "I know that I'm not exactly in a friendly camp here."

"That's your doing," Malone said, "not ours."

"Okay," Cosner said, "so I'm not the friendliest person in the world, but that doesn't mean I want to see anyone hurt—especially not me."

"What are you talking about?" Clint asked.

"Three guys jumped on me tonight, right in the street. They were going to give me a beating!"

"How did you get away?" Day asked. He remembered his own close call the other night.

"I don't know," Cosner said. "I think I went crazy. The next thing I knew I was running away. I guess I just outran them."

"And came here?" Malone said.

Cosner shrugged. "I figured this was the safest place." He looked at Day and said, "I didn't expect to find you here. Guess you felt the same way, huh?"

"I was invited."

"Oh," said Cosner, "I see."

He looked at each of them in turn—Clint, Malone, Day, and Dee—and then began to stand up.

"I can see I'm not welcome here. I guess I'll be going then."

"Sit down, Keith Cosner," Dee said. "You're right—you're not welcome and I think you're a horrible man—but I wouldn't even send *you* out to be killed."

Cosner sat down and looked at Dee with his mouth open.

"Keith," Clint said, "I think you've just been invited."

THIRTY-SIX

The next morning Clint, Malone, Day, and Cosner went into town early. Malone and Day took the buggy. Cosner rode the horse he had ridden the night before, and Clint took Duke. It was good to give him some exercise.

They went first to Doug DeWitt's boardinghouse, where they outlined Clint's plan. He agreed and insisted on going with them. He crowded onto the buggy with Malone and Johnny Day.

When they pulled up in front of Clifton Davies's house Clint was impressed. He had seen homes like this one in New Orleans and other cities in Louisiana. It seemed to have been modeled after the grand homes of the South, complete with white columns in front.

They all crowded around the front door, and DeWitt was the one who utilized the brass knocker.

The door was opened by a tall, white-haired man wearing a dark suit.

"Can I help you?"

148

"Henry, we'd like to see Mr. Davies," DeWitt said.

The servant looked at each of them in turn and then asked, "All of you?"

"Yeah, all of us, Henry," Cosner said. "Now, let us in and tell him we're here."

Henry gave Cosner a look that said he didn't like the man any more than anyone else did.

"Come in, gentlemen," he said finally. "I'll tell Mr. Davies you're here."

He told Mr. Davies they were there and then ushered them all into Davies's office.

"What's going on, gentlemen?" Davies asked. He was still in his pajamas, and he wore a silk robe over them. "DeWitt?"

"Uh, maybe I'd better let Clint explain, Mr. Davies. He's sort of in charge."

"Clint?"

"That'd be me," Clint said.

"Ah, Mr. Adams," Davies said. "I very much enjoyed watching you work the other day."

"Work? Oh, you mean *pitch*. Yes, thank you."

Cosner made a sound, but everyone ignored him.

"Suppose you tell me what brings all of you here this early in the morning, Mr. Adams."

Clint told him about Jerry Cole, the attempt on Johnny Day, the one on Malone, the one on him, and Cosner's close call just the night before.

"The attempt on you seems to have been a little more serious," Davies said. "Are you sure it's in line with the others?"

"If we were in Texas, Oklahoma, or Arizona, I'd say no, Mr. Davies, but here in Cedar Rapids, I believe it's part and parcel with the others."

"Well," Davies said, "I don't have enough chairs here, but some of you should sit down."

Davies seated himself behind his desk. There were two other chairs in the room, and Clint and Doug DeWitt took those. The three oldest men in the room were now sitting down.

"Apparently," Davies said after a moment, "someone doesn't want us to win tomorrow. They're trying to injure the team's best players."

"That's what Clint figured," DeWitt said.

"Would you have any idea who's doing it, Mr. Davies?" Clint asked.

"Of course I would," Davies said. "Obviously, some of my peers have come to the conclusion that the Bulls are mine. They're trying to keep me out of the league."

"Uh, which of your peers would you suspect?"

"Well," he said, "three of the owners voted against me, so it would have to be either Kenneth Selma—he owns the Chicago White Stockings—or Peter McBain—he owns the New York Giants—or William Ryker, who owns the Red Stockings, the team you're playing tomorrow."

"Then it must be him," Clint said.

"Well, I agree," Davies said, "but not for that reason."

"What reason, then?" Clint asked.

"It's his style," Davies said. "Oh, he'd have Selma and McBain's approval to do something, but Ryker would come up with a plan like this. He'd have his man, David Drake, arrange it."

"Ryker and Drake," Clint said. "Thank you, Mr. Davies." Clint started to get up.

"Sit back down, young man."

Clint stopped, half standing, and looked at Davies.

"Sit."

Clint sat down.

"Where are you going?"

"To talk to Mr. Ryker and Mr. Drake."

"You don't even know where they're staying."

Clint realized that Davies was right.

"Do you?" he asked.

"Of course."

"Will you tell me?"

"No."

"Why not?"

"Because I don't want you going over there now and killing them."

"I have no intention of killing them."

"Or even sending them to jail," Davies said. "Oh, no. I want William Ryker to watch the Bulls beat his Red Stockings, and then you can have him."

"How are we gonna beat them if they injure our players?" DeWitt asked. "They have to be stopped now."

"No they don't," Davies said. "You can have them after the games, but not before."

"Well," DeWitt said, "what do we do tonight to keep everyone safe?"

"Bring them here."

DeWitt stared.

"Bring them here?"

"That's right."

"The whole team?"

"Every last man," Davies said. "We have plenty of room. Tomorrow we can all go to the game from here."

"Together?"

"Together," Davies said. "I still don't own the Bulls officially, so there's nothing they can do to stop us from playing."

DeWitt turned and looked at Clint.

"What do you think?"

"I kind of like the idea of this Ryker watching us beat his team," Clint said. "I like the idea."

DeWitt, looking baffled, threw his hands in the air and said, "Well, all right then. Let's go get the rest of the team."

"I'm staying here, where it's safe," Cosner said.

"Keith, you'll come with me, while Malone and Day go with Clint."

"Oh no," Cosner said. "There's some guys out there looking to hurt me. I'm staying here."

"Mr. Cosner," Davies said, "I have always known you to be arrogant and selfish. Are you now going to show me that you are a coward as well?"

"A what?"

"I believe you heard me, sir."

Cosner stared at Davies for a few moments, then said to DeWitt, "Well, what the hell are you waiting for, Skip? Let's go get the rest of the team."

DeWitt and Clint stood up.

"As we find them we'll send them over here," Clint said to Davies.

"Henry and Olivia will see to their needs," Davies said. "Uh, I assume it will take most of the day to round them up."

"I expect it will," Clint said.

"When you have all returned, we will serve everyone dinner," Davies said.

"Fine," Clint said.

"Mr. Adams," Davies said as Clint was going out the door last. Clint stopped and turned. "After dinner, I'd be very pleased if you joined me for a drink and a talk."

"All right, sir," Clint said. "I'll do that."

THIRTY-SEVEN

It took most of the day but they finally had the entire Cedar Rapids Bulls collected at Clifton Davies's house. Clint and DeWitt had decided to simply tell the players that Davies wanted to give them all dinner and then put them up in his house overnight for luck. They didn't know how many of the players actually believed the story, but that didn't matter. What mattered was that they had all the players under one roof, and, short of bombing the house, there was nothing anyone could do about it.

"Bombing the house?" DeWitt asked, looking at Clint.

"I think that would be a little drastic," Clint said, "for anyone."

"Mr. Davies wants to see you after dinner," DeWitt said. "Maybe you could ask him if it *would* be a little drastic for this feller Ryker—just to be on the safe side."

"I'll mention it to him," Clint promised.

After dinner Clint went to Davies's office and found his host sitting behind his desk with a glass of sherry. He had also poured one for Clint. It was sitting on the edge of the desk on Clint's side.

"Ah, Mr. Adams," Davies said. "Sit, please. This is excellent sherry."

"Thank you," Clint said. He sat down and tried the sherry. Davies was right: It was excellent.

"So tell me," Davies said, "which of your lives do you like better?"

"I beg your pardon?"

"Actually, I should simply ask you how you like pitching baseball, and if you have any intention of staying with it."

"I haven't really pitched in a real game yet," Clint said. "Also, all this hubbub is sort of taking the enjoyment out of the game for me."

"Don't worry about the hubbub," Davies said. "After we beat the Red Stockings it will be over. We'll be in the league, and no one will be able to do anything about it."

"And if we lose?"

Davies frowned, as if he didn't even like the suggestion, but he said, "Then it will still be all over. Either way, the matter will be resolved."

"I suppose so."

"I understand you're pitching the second game."

"Yes, sir."

"How do you think you'll do?"

"Well, if my lack of knowledge of the fundamentals doesn't hurt me, we should do fine."

"The game will come to you with time—depending on how long you stay with it. Ah, do you have any idea of how long that will be?"

"Not really. Is it important?"

"Well, once I take over the team, I'll be paying the players. I have contracts with all of the players, all signed and sealed—except for you."

So that's what this was about: A contract negotiation.

"Uh, I don't think we need worry about that, Mr. Davies."

"You'll have to be paid for your work."

"Why don't we just work it out on a day-to-day basis?" Clint suggested.

"Well, that sounds fair. Suppose we talk about how much—"

"Let's not."

"I beg your pardon?"

Clint stood up and set the empty sherry glass down on the desk. "Why don't you just pay me what you think I'm worth?"

"I . . . really have nothing to base that on at this point."

"Well then, wait until the games with the Red Stockings are over and then make up your mind. I'm sure you'll be fair."

"How can you be so sure?" Davies asked.

Clint was walking to the door, and he turned to answer the question. "I don't see that you have any reason not to be. Good night, Mr. Davis."

Davies watched Clint leave the room, then sat back in his chair, sipped his sherry, and uttered a single word.

"Extraordinary!"

"You what?" William Ryker asked David Drake.

"We can't find any of the team."

"What happened to them?"

"I don't know," Drake said. "They've . . . disappeared."

"How can that be?"

"I don't know."

"Stop saying that, Drake," Ryker said. "I don't pay you to say 'I don't know.' Find out."

"Yes, sir," Drake said. "I'll find out."

But he never did.

•   •   •

Drake returned to the hotel later and reported his failure.

"That's all right, Drake," Ryker said.

Drake was taken aback by the ease with which Ryker had accepted the news.

"It is?"

"Sure it is," Ryker said, "because I figured out where they have to be."

"Where?"

"Just get some men who are good with a rifle," Ryker said. "We're going to give that whole team a surprise tomorrow morning. By the time they get to the baseball stadium tomorrow, they aren't going to be in any condition to play baseball."

THIRTY-EIGHT

DeWitt and Clint roused all the players the next morning. Davies had already arranged transportation for all of them, and the buggies were lined up out in front of the house.

"What's the matter?" DeWitt asked Clint.

Clint had been standing off to one side, watching the players load into the buggies.

"I was just thinking."

"About what?"

"How easy it would be for somebody to ambush this wagon train."

"What?" DeWitt asked. "Ambush?"

Clint was rubbing his jaw. "Doug, is there anybody on this team who can shoot?"

"Probably," DeWitt said.

"I know Malone can shoot. I need about two other men—that's all."

"I'll pull them out."

At that point Clifton Davies came out the front door.

"Mr. Davies, I need some help," said Clint.

"With what, Clint?"

"Well, I need three rifles and three horses."

"What for?"

Clint explained what he was afraid might happen.

"For that to occur, Ryker would have to know that you boys spent the night here."

"Or guess," Clint said. "How hard would it be for him to guess?"

Davies thought about it for a moment, then rubbed his jaw. "Not hard. I'll get you the rifles. You can get the horses from the stable out back."

"All right."

DeWitt came over, trailing Sam Malone and two other men behind him. Clint dug up their names: Billy Wallace and Archie Ray.

"Clint, you know Billy and Archie?"

"How are you boys doing?" Clint asked. "I understand you can shoot."

"We hunt together," Wallace said. "Archie's a better shot than I am."

"Have you fellers ever shot at another man?"

Wallace and Ray exchanged a glance, and then both of them shook their heads.

"Sam? I know you haven't."

"No."

"Could you?" Clint asked. He knew that was a foolish question. No man knew if he could shoot at another man until the time came.

"Never mind," Clint said. "We're going to get some horses and go on ahead of the buggies."

"What for?" Archie Ray asked.

"Just in case somebody's waiting up ahead with a little surprise."

"What kind of surprise?" Wallace asked.

Clint looked at Malone and said, "Explain the situation to them, Sam." He turned to DeWitt and said, "Don't let anyone leave until we get a head start."

"All right."

"I'll get the horses."

David Drake and five other men were waiting along a deserted strip of road where the buggies would have to pass on the way to the stadium from Clifton Davies's house. Ryker had told Drake to personally supervise this operation.

"What are we supposed to do, specifically?" Drake had asked.

"Put a scare into them so that their hands don't stop shaking, not even during the game," Ryker had said.

"Do we kill any of them?" Drake had asked.

Ryker had shrugged his shoulders and said simply, "if that's what it takes."

"Remember," Drake told his men now, "if you have a clear shot at someone, take it."

"There's extra money in it if we kill someone, right?" one of the men asked.

Drake gave the man a hard stare. "It's not a bounty; it's simply to compensate you."

The man who spoke shrugged. He didn't care what they called it. All he knew was that he got paid extra if he killed someone.

Drake deployed his men, three on either side of the road, and they waited.

"Why aren't we on the road?" Archie Ray asked.

"Because the men we're after will be watching the road," Clint explained.

"Clint," Billy Wallace said, "I don't know if I can kill another man."

"Hopefully we won't have to," Clint said. "Maybe when they experience some resistance they'll just turn and run. It doesn't matter. All we want to do is make sure the team gets to the stadium safely. If you want, you can fire over their heads—but keep your own heads down."

"I'm not firing over anyone's head if they're shooting at my head," Sam Malone said.

"Let's just wait and see what happens, Sam," Clint said.

THIRTY-NINE

"Slow down," Clint said.

The other three were riding behind him, and they slowed at his command.

"What's wrong?" Malone asked.

"Wait here."

Clint rode on without answering Malone's question. What was wrong was that he thought he saw something, or he sensed something, up ahead. That would have been hard to explain to Sam Malone and the others.

Clint rode ahead a ways. He had taken Malone and the other two out of town, and they were now riding on the outskirts of Cedar Rapids. There was a stretch of road ahead that Clint remembered from the trip to Davies's house. It was almost deserted, with just a few houses along the way, and if Clint were right then it was a good place for an ambush.

He dismounted and left Duke alone while he walked ahead, parallel with the road. Sure enough, he saw three men waiting off the road, on an incline that was not steep, though steep enough to hide them from sight. If Clint were setting up an ambush, he'd have put the same amount of men on the other side of the road as well.

He walked back to Duke and then rode back to where he'd left Malone, Wallace, and Ray.

He told them what he had seen ahead and what he figured.

"Sam, take Ray and ride on this side of the road. About two hundred yards up dismount and walk along for about another twenty yards and you'll see them. They'll have their backs to you. Try to get up behind them without them seeing you."

"And if they do see us?"

Clint shrugged. "Hit the ground and start shooting. Hopefully they'll start running."

"And if they don't?" Archie Ray asked.

"Then it'll be up to you," Clint said. "You can shoot at them, or you can be the ones to run."

"We won't run," Malone said. "Come on, Archie."

"What are we gonna do?" Wallace asked.

"We're going to work the other side of the road," Clint said. "There should be three men there as well."

"And if there ain't?"

"Then we'll help Sam and Archie," Clint said, "but they'll be there."

"How can you be so sure?"

"Because if it was me, I'd put them there. Come on."

Where Clint and Billy Wallace were riding it wasn't as wide open as on the other side. They were riding along behind some homes when Clint called a halt.

"We'll leave the horses here."

Wallace dismounted and followed Clint, nervously fingering the rifle he was holding.

They moved along as quietly as they could—Clint quieter than Wallace—until Clint could see the backs of three men.

"There they are."

"Now what?" Wallace asked.

"We work our way up on them. Hopefully we'll get the drop on them with no shooting."

"I hope so," Wallace said, and he tried to swallow a lump that had formed in his throat.

Clint knew Wallace was nervous, so he was prepared to do all the shooting, if it came to that.

They were moving up on the three men when they suddenly heard shooting from the other side of the road.

"Damn," Clint said.

Wallace, panicked by the sound of shooting, shouldered his rifle and started shooting as quickly as he could lever new rounds into the chamber.

"Billy, stop!"

Wallace was beyond stopping, and he wasn't hitting anything. What he was doing, though, was causing the three men to scatter. His wild fire was falling all around them.

Clint watched a dark-haired man who was better dressed than the other two. He also moved like he knew where he was going, and he wasn't just diving for the nearest cover.

The three men started to fire back, and Clint grabbed Wallace by the back of the belt and pulled him down to the ground.

"D—did I hit anybody?" he asked.

"Not a one," Clint said. "Reload and cover me."

"How do I do that?"

"Just do what you were just doing," Clint said, "but do it from a prone position—and don't worry about hitting anyone."

"Right."

"Wait a minute," Clint said, putting his hand on Wallace's arm. "Just worry about not hitting me, okay?"

"Okay," Wallace said, nodding his head jerkily.

"You reloaded?"

"Yes."

"Then start firing."

Wallace began to fire, and Clint got up and started running toward them in a crouch.

One man saw Clint and stood up to get a clear shot. Clint fired first, and the man spun away and out of sight. A second man, seeing what had happened, turned to run, and damned if one of Wallace's shot didn't wing him. Clint saw the man's gun go flying and saw him grab his gun arm.

That left the dark-haired man. Clint looked around and saw the man, working his way along the road and trying to get away. He started after him, aware that there were still shots being fired from the other side of the road. He turned and waved Wallace on. He hoped the man would know enough to go to the aid of Malone and Ray.

Clint followed the dark-haired man and suddenly knew that he was moving toward a nearby house. He must have had a horse waiting there. As Clint ran, he ejected the empty shells from his gun and slid in new ones.

Clint's legs were longer than the other man's and he began closing the ground between them. The man looked over his shoulder every so often, which also slowed him down. Finally, the man gave up the idea of outrunning Clint and turned to face him. As he did so his foot slipped on the incline and went out from under him. He rolled a short distance, and when he came to a stop he started looking around for his gun.

"Don't," Clint said, having reached him by then.

The man looked up at Clint. He had located his gun and was now alternating between Clint and the gun, which was about two feet to his left.

"You Drake?" Clint asked.

Drake frowned, obviously puzzled by the fact that Clint knew his name.

He nodded.

"I'm Adams."

Drake's eyebrows went up, and he suddenly gave up on the gun. Clint could see the resignation in his posture.

"Get up," he said.

Drake got to his feet, not bothering to brush off his suit. If he was going to die, it didn't matter.

"You got a horse near here?" Clint asked.

"Behind that house."

"A rifle there?"

"Yes."

"Go to your horse and ride away. Don't try to come back with the rifle, because I'll kill you."

"You're letting me go?" Drake asked, surprised.

"My guess is that you're following orders."

"That's right."

"Go back and tell your boss, Ryker, to be sure to get to the stadium in time. I wouldn't want him to miss the game."

"I'll tell him," Drake said.

"Then go and find yourself a new employer. This one's likely to get you killed."

"He pays well."

"Well enough to die for?"

Drake thought a moment, then said, "Nobody pays that well."

"Go," Clint said.

"I'm gone."

Drake turned and started running toward the house. Clint turned and walked up to stand on the road. Off in the distance, he saw the line of buggies approaching. Between him and the buggies he saw Malone, Wallace, and Ray standing in the road with a few other men who had their hands up.

Clint holstered his gun and said, "Play ball."

EPILOGUE

From *The Cedar Rapids Gazette:*

Cedar Rapids has a National League baseball team!

The Cedar Rapids Bulls defeated the Cincinnati Red Stockings *twice* yesterday, to earn a position in the National Baseball League. This arrangement was made with the National League owners, after a vote of all eight owners resulted in a 5–3 decision to give the Bulls a chance.

Former professional pitcher Keith Cosner pitched the first game, limiting the Red Stockings to three hits in a 2–1 Bulls win. Catcher Johnny Day had two run-scoring hits.

The second game was started by unknown Clint Duke, who pitched the first five innings, giving up no hits and striking out every batter he faced. He left the game with a mysterious injury that seemed to have disappeared after the game. Local boy Sam Malone pitched a perfect final four innings, as he and Duke combined on a 3–0 no-hitter.

After the game Clint Duke was unavail-
able for comment, but we did talk with
Keith Cosner, Sam Malone, and Manager
Doug DeWitt. . . .

Dee Malone rolled over in bed and looked at Clint. They were in a Cedar Rapids hotel, finishing what they had started in the hayloft before saying goodbye.

She was holding the newspaper, folded to the story about the baseball games the day before. "Tell me," she said, "about this mysterious injury that forced Doug to put Sam into the game."

"I didn't want the Bulls getting into the league without Sam's help," Clint said. "When it looked like we might win both games, I faked the injury to get him into the game."

Dee slid on top of Clint, her breasts crushed against his chest, and kissed him deeply.

"You're a rare kind of man, Clint Adams. Oh, and what's this business about Clint Duke?"

"I just didn't want my real name in the newspapers. You never know who might read it."

"What's going to happen to William Ryker?"

"Nothing, I guess."

"That doesn't sound fair."

"You have to remember what a wealthy man he is," Clint said. "The wealthy get away with a lot in this world. That's just the way it is."

"Well, at least he can't do anything about the Bulls being in the league."

"No," Clint said, "that's done. Maybe we should just leave it up to Mr. Davies to see that Ryker gets what's coming to him. At least he's wealthy enough to try to do something about it."

"Tell me something," she said.

"What?"

"Aren't you the least bit tempted to stay and travel with the team for a while before you go back west?"

He slid his hands down her bare back and cupped her big, smooth buttocks.

"I'm a little tempted," he said, "but I think it's time for me to go home."

"A pity."

"Yes," he said, squeezing her ass, "it is."

"But at least we made the time to finish what we started, huh?"

He smiled, kissed her, and said, "And we're not finished yet. I'm not leaving until tomorrow."

"Tomorrow, huh?" she asked, smiling.

"Do you think Sam will miss you at the farm today and tonight?"

"He might," he said, lifting her hips, "but he's a big boy. He'll get along."

She reached between them for his rigid penis and slid him into her, taking him slowly so that her heat crept up his length.

"Come on," he whispered into her ear, "let's see how long it takes us to reach home plate."

Watch for

THE OREGON STRANGLER

116th novel in the exciting GUNSMITH series
from Jove

Coming in August!

GILES TIPPETTE

Author of the best-selling WILSON YOUNG
SERIES, BAD NEWS, and CROSS FIRE

is back with his most exciting
Western adventure yet!

JAILBREAK

Time is running out for Justa Williams, owner of the Half-
Moon Ranch in West Texas. His brother Norris is being
held in a Mexican jail, and neither bribes nor threats can
free him.

Now, with the help of a dozen kill-crazy Mexican *banditos*,
Justa aims to blast Norris out. But the worst is yet to come:
a hundred-mile chase across the Mexican desert with fifty
federales in hot pursuit.

The odds of reaching the Texas border are a million to nothing . . . and if the Williams brothers don't watch their backs,
the road to freedom could turn into the road to hell!

Turn the page for an exciting preview of

Jailbreak
by
Giles Tippette

On sale now, wherever Jove Books are sold!

At supper Norris, my middle brother, said, "I think we got some trouble on that five thousand acres down on the border near Laredo."

He said it serious, which is the way Norris generally says everything. I was wrestling with the steak Buttercup, our cook, had turned into rawhide and said, "What are you talking about? How could we have trouble on land lying idle?"

He said, "I got word from town this afternoon that a telegram had come in from a friend of ours down there. He says we got some kind of squatters taking up residence on the place."

My youngest brother, Ben, put his fork down and said, incredulously, "*That* five thousand acres? Hell, it ain't nothing but rocks and cactus and sand. Why in hell would anyone want to squat on that worthless piece of nothing?"

Norris just shook his head. "I don't know. But that's what the telegram said. Came from Jack Cole. And if anyone ought to know what's going on down there it would be him."

I thought about it and it didn't make a bit of sense. I was
Justa Williams, and my family, my two brothers and myself
and our father, Howard, occupied a considerable ranch
called the Half-Moon down along the Gulf of Mexico in
Matagorda Country, Texas. It was some of the best grazing
land in the state and we had one of the best herds of purebred
and crossbred cattle in that part of the country. In short we
were pretty well-to-do.

But that didn't make us any the less ready to be stolen
from, if indeed that was the case. The five thousand acres
Norris had been talking about had come to us through a
trade our father had made some years before. We'd never
made any use of the land mainly because, as Ben had said,
it was pretty worthless, because it was a good two hundred
miles from our ranch headquarters. On a few occasions we'd
bought cattle in Mexico and then used the acreage to hold
small groups on while we made up a herd. But other than
that, it lay mainly forgotten.

I frowned. "Norris, this doesn't make a damn bit of sense.
Right after supper send a man into Blessing with a return
wire for Jack asking him if he's certain. What the hell kind
of squatting could anybody be doing on that land?"

Ben said, "Maybe they're raisin' watermelons." He
laughed.

I said, "They could raise melons, but there damn sure
wouldn't be no water in them."

Norris said, "Well, it bears looking into." He got up,
throwing his napkin on the table. "I'll go write out that
telegram."

I watched him go, dressed, as always, in his town clothes.
Norris was the businessman in the family. He'd been sent
down to the University at Austin and had got considerable
learning about the ins and outs of banking and land deals
and all the other parts of our business that didn't directly

involve the ranch. At the age of twenty-nine I'd been the
boss of the operation a good deal longer than I cared to
think about. It had been thrust upon me by our father when
I wasn't much more than twenty. He'd said he'd wanted
me to take over while he was still strong enough to help
me out of my mistakes and I reckoned that was partly true.
But it had just seemed that after our mother had died the
life had sort of gone out of him. He'd been one of the
earliest settlers, taking up the land not long after Texas had
become a republic in 1845 I figured all the years of fighting
Indians and then Yankees and scalawags and carpetbaggers
and cattle thieves had taken their toll on him. Then a few
years back he'd been nicked in the lungs by a bullet that
should never have been allowed to heed his way and it
had thrown an extra strain on his heart. He was pushing
seventy and he still had plenty of head on his shoulders,
but mostly all he did now was sit around in his rocking
chair and stare out over the cattle and land business he'd
built. Not to say that I didn't go to him for advice when
the occasion demanded. I did, and mostly I took it.

Buttercup came in just then and sat down at the end of
the table with a cup of coffee. He was near as old as Dad
and almost completely worthless. But he'd been one of the
first hands that Dad had hired and he'd been kept on even
after he couldn't sit a horse anymore. The problem was
he'd elected himself cook, and that was the sorriest day
our family had ever seen. There were two Mexican women
hired to cook for the twelve riders we kept full time, but
Buttercup insisted on cooking for the family.

Mainly, I think, because he thought he was one of the
family. A notion we could never completely dissuade him
from.

So he sat there, about two days of stubble on his face,
looking as scrawny as a pecked-out rooster, sweat running

down his face, his apron a mess. He said, wiping his forearm across his forehead, "Boy, it shore be hot in there. You boys shore better be glad you ain't got no business takes you in that kitchen."

Ben said, in a loud mutter, "I wish you didn't either."

Ben, at twenty-five, was easily the best man with a horse or a gun that I had ever seen. His only drawback was that he was hotheaded and he tended to act first and think later. That ain't a real good combination for someone that could go on the prod as fast as Ben. When I had argued with Dad about taking over as boss, suggesting instead that Norris, with his education, was a much better choice, Dad had simply said, "Yes, in some ways. But he can't handle Ben. You can. You can handle Norris, too. But none of them can handle you."

Well, that hadn't been exactly true. If Dad had wished it I would have taken orders from Norris even though he was two years younger than me. But the logic in Dad's line of thinking had been that the Half-Moon and our cattle business was the lodestone of all our businesses and only I could run that. He had been right. In the past I'd imported purebred Whiteface and Hereford cattle from up North, bred them to our native Longhorns and produced cattle that would bring twice as much at market as the horse-killing, all-bone, all-wild Longhorns. My neighbors had laughed at me at first, claiming those square little purebreds would never make it in our Texas heat. But they'd been wrong and, one by one, they'd followed the example of the Half-Moon.

Buttercup was setting up to take off on another one of his long-winded harrangues about how it had been in the "old days" so I quickly got up, excusing myself, and went into the big office we used for sitting around in as well as a place of business. Norris was at the desk composing his telegram so I poured myself out a whiskey and sat down. I didn't want to hear about my trouble over some worthless five thousand acres of borderland. In fact I didn't want to hear about any troubles of any kind. I was just two weeks short of getting married, married to a lady I'd been courting off and on for five years, and I was mighty anxious that nothing come up to interfere with our plans. Her name was Nora Parker and her daddy owned and run the general mercantile in our nearest town, Blessing. I'd almost lost her once before to a Kansas City drummer. She'd finally gotten tired of waiting on me, waiting until the ranch didn't occupy all my time, and almost run off with a smooth-talking Kansas City drummer that called on her daddy in the harness trade. But she'd come to her senses in time and got off the train in Texarkana and returned home.

But even then it had been a close thing. I, along with my men and brothers and help from some of our neighbors, had been involved with stopping a huge herd of illegal cattle being driven up from Mexico from crossing our range and infecting our cattle with tick fever which could have wiped us all out. I tell you it had been a bloody business. We'd lost four good men and had to kill at least a half dozen on the other side. Fact of the business was I'd come about as close as I ever had to getting killed myself, and that was going some for the sort of rough-and-tumble life I'd led.

Nora had almost quit me over it, saying she just couldn't take the uncertainty. But in the end, she'd stuck by me. That had been the year before, 1896, and I'd convinced her that civilized law was coming to the country, but until it did, we that had been there before might have to take things into our own hands from time to time.

She'd seen that and had understood. I loved her and she loved me and that was enough to overcome any of the troubles we were still likely to encounter from day to day.

So I was giving Norris a pretty sour look as he finished his telegram and sent for a hired hand to ride it into Blessing, seven miles away. I said, "Norris, let's don't make a big fuss about this. That land ain't even crossed my mind in at least a couple of years. Likely we got a few Mexican families squatting down there and trying to scratch out a few acres of corn."

Norris gave me his businessman's look. He said, "It's our land, Justa. And if we allow anyone to squat on it for long enough or put up a fence they can lay claim. That's the law. My job is to see that we protect what we have, not give it away."

I sipped at my whiskey and studied Norris. In his town clothes he didn't look very impressive. He'd inherited more from our mother than from Dad so he was not as wide shouldered and slim-hipped as Ben and me. But I knew him to be a good, strong, dependable man in any kind of fight. Of course he wasn't that good with a gun, but then Ben and I weren't all that good with books like he was. But I said, just to jolly him a bit, "Norris, I do believe you are running to suet. I may have to put you out with Ben working the horse herd and work a little of that fat off you."

Naturally it got his goat. Norris had always envied Ben and me a little. I was just over six foot and weighed right around one hundred and ninety. I had inherited my daddy's big hands and big shoulders. Ben was almost a copy of me except he was about a size smaller. Norris said, "I weigh the same as I have for the last five years. If it's any of your business."

I said, as if I was being serious, "Must be them sack suits you wear. What they do, pad them around the middle?"

He said, "Why don't you just go to hell."

After he'd stomped out of the room I got the bottle of whiskey and an extra glass and went down to Dad's room. It had been one of his bad days and he'd taken to bed right after lunch. Strictly speaking he wasn't supposed to have no whiskey, but I watered him down a shot every now and then and it didn't seem to do him no harm.

He was sitting up when I came in the room. I took a moment to fix him a little drink, using some water out of his pitcher, then handed him the glass and sat down in the easy chair by the bed. I told him what Norris had reported and asked what he thought.

He took a sip of his drink and shook his head. "Beats all I ever heard." he said. "I took that land in trade for a bad debt some fifteen, twenty years ago. I reckon I'd of been money ahead if I'd of hung on to the bad debt. That land won't even raise weeds, well as I remember, and Noah was in on the last rain that fell on the place."

We had considerable amounts of land spotted around the state as a result of this kind of trade or that. It was Norris's business to keep up with their management. I was just bringing this to Dad's attention more out of boredom and impatience for my wedding day to arrive than anything else.

I said, "Well, it's a mystery to me. How you feeling?"

He half smiled. "Old." Then he looked into his glass. "And I never liked watered whiskey. Pour me a dollop of the straight stuff in here."

I said, "Now, Howard. You know—"

He cut me off. "If I wanted somebody to argue with I'd send for Buttercup. Now do like I told you."

I did, but I felt guilty about it. He took the slug of whiskey down in one pull. Then he leaned his head back on the pillow and said, "Aaaaah. I don't give a damn what that horse doctor says, ain't nothing makes a man feel as good inside as a shot of the best."

I felt sorry for him laying there. He'd always led just the kind of life he wanted—going where he wanted, doing what he wanted, having what he set out to get. And now he was reduced to being a semi-invalid. But one thing that showed the strength that was still in him was that you *never* heard him complain. He said, "How's the cattle?"

I said, "They're doing all right, but I tell you we could do with a little of Noah's flood right now. All this heat and no rain is curing the grass off way ahead of time. If it doesn't let up we'll be feeding hay by late September, early October. And that will play hell on our supply. Could be we won't have enough to last through the winter. Norris thinks we ought to sell off five hundred head or so, but the market is doing poorly right now. I'd rather chance the weather than take a sure beating by selling off."

He sort of shrugged and closed his eyes. The whiskey was relaxing him. He said, "You're the boss."

"Yeah," I said. "Damn my luck."

I wandered out of the back of the house. Even though it was nearing seven o'clock of the evening it was still good and hot. Off in the distance, about a half a mile away, I could see the outline of the house I was building for Nora and myself. It was going to be a close thing to get it finished by our wedding day. Not having any riders to spare for the project, I'd imported a building contractor from Galveston, sixty miles away. He'd arrived with a half a dozen Mexican laborers and a few skilled masons and they'd set up a little tent city around the place. The contractor had gone back to Galveston to fetch more materials, leaving his Mexicans behind. I walked along idly, hoping he wouldn't forget that the job wasn't done. He had some of my money, but not near what he'd get when he finished the job.

Just then Ray Hays came hurrying across the back lot toward me. Ray was kind of a special case for me. The only problem with that was that he knew it and wasn't a bit above taking advantage of the situation. Once, a few years past, he'd saved my life by going against an evil man that he was working for at the time, an evil man who meant to have my life. In gratitude I'd given Ray a good job at the Half-Moon, letting him work directly under Ben, who was responsible for the horse herd. He was a good, steady man and a good man with a gun. He was also fair company. When he wasn't talking.

He came churning up to me, mopping his brow. He said, "Lordy, boss, it is—"

I said, "Hays, if you say it's hot I'm going to knock you down."

He gave me a look that was a mixture of astonishment and hurt. He said, "Why, whatever for?"

I said, "*Everybody* knows it's hot. Does every son of a bitch you run into have to make mention of the fact?"

His brow furrowed. "Well, I never thought of it that way. I 'spect you are right. Goin' down to look at yore house?"

I shook my head. "No. It makes me nervous to see how far they've got to go. I can't see any way it'll be ready on time."

He said, "Miss Nora ain't gonna like that."

I gave him a look. "I guess you felt forced to say that."

He looked down. "Well, maybe she won't mind."

I said, grimly, "The hell she won't. She'll think I did it a-purpose."

"Aw, she wouldn't."

"Naturally you know so much about it, Hays. Why don't you tell me a few other things about her."

"I was jest tryin' to lift yore spirits, boss."

I said, "You keep trying to lift my spirits and I'll put you on the haying crew."

He looked horrified. No real cowhand wanted any work he couldn't do from the back of his horse. Haying was a hot, hard, sweaty job done either afoot or from a wagon seat. We generally brought in contract Mexican labor to handle ours. But I'd been known in the past to discipline a cowhand by giving him a few days on the hay gang. Hays said, "Boss, now I never meant nothin'. I swear. You know me, my mouth gets to runnin' sometimes. I swear I'm gonna watch it."

I smiled. Hays always made me smile. He was so easily buffaloed. He had it soft at the Half-Moon and he knew it and didn't want to take any chances on losing a good thing.

I lit up a cigarillo and watched dusk settle in over the coastal plains. It wasn't but three miles to Matagorda Bay and it was quiet enough I felt like I could almost hear the waves breaking on the shore. Somewhere in the distance a mama cow bawled for her calf. The spring crop were near about weaned by now, but there were still a few mamas that wouldn't cut the apron strings. I stood there reflecting on how peaceful things had been of late. It suited me just fine. All I wanted was to get my house finished, marry Nora and never handle another gun so long as I lived.

The peace and quiet were short-lived. Within twenty-four hours we'd had a return telegram from Jack Cole. It said:

YOUR LAND OCCUPIED BY TEN TO TWELVE MEN STOP CAN'T BE SURE WHAT THEY'RE DOING BECAUSE THEY RUN STRANGERS OFF STOP APPEAR TO HAVE A GOOD MANY CATTLE GATHERED STOP APPEAR TO BE FENCING STOP ALL I KNOW STOP

I read the telegram twice and then I said, "Why this is crazy as hell! That land wouldn't support fifty head of cattle."

We were all gathered in the big office. Even Dad was there, sitting in his rocking chair. I looked up at him. "What do you make of this, Howard?"

He shook his big, old head of white hair. "Beats the hell out off me, Justa. I can't figure it."

Ben said, "Well, I don't see where it has to be figured. I'll take five men and go down there and run them off. I don't care what they're doing. They ain't got no business on our land."

I said, "Take it easy, Ben. Aside from the fact you don't need to be getting into any more fights this year, I can't spare you or five men. The way this grass is drying up we've got to keep drifting those cattle."

Norris said, "No, Ben is right. We can't have such affairs going on with our property. But we'll handle it within the law. I'll simply take the train down there, hire a good lawyer and have the matter settled by the sheriff. Shouldn't take but a few days."

Well, there wasn't much I could say to that. We couldn't very well let people take advantage of us, but I still hated to be without Norris's services even for a few days. On matters other than the ranch he was the expert, and it didn't seem like there was a day went by that some financial question didn't come up that only he could answer. I said, "Are you sure you can spare yourself for a few days?"

He thought for a moment and then nodded. "I don't see why not. I've just moved most of our available cash into short-term municipal bonds in Galveston. The market is looking all right and everything appears fine at the bank. I can't think of anything that might come up."

I said, "All right. But you just keep this in mind. You are not a gun hand. You are not a fighter. I do not want you going anywhere near those people, whoever they are. You do it legal and let the sheriff handle the eviction. Is that understood?"

He kind of swelled up, resenting the implication that he couldn't handle himself. The biggest trouble I'd had through the years when trouble had come up had been keeping Norris out of it. Why he couldn't just be content to be a wagon load of brains was more than I could understand. He said, "Didn't you just hear me say I intended to go through a lawyer and the sheriff? Didn't I just say that?"

I said, "I wanted to be sure you heard yourself."

He said. "Nothing wrong with my hearing. Nor my approach to this matter. You seem to constantly be taken with the idea that I'm always looking for a fight. I think you've got the wrong brother. I use logic."

"Yeah?" I said. "You remember when that guy kicked you in the balls when they were holding guns on us? And then we chased them twenty miles and finally caught them?"

He looked away. "That has nothing to do with this."

"Yeah?" I said, enjoying myself. "And here's this guy, shot all to hell. And what was it you insisted on doing?"

Ben laughed, but Norris wouldn't say anything.

I said, "Didn't you insist on us standing him up so you could kick him in the balls? Didn't you?"

He sort of growled, "Oh, go to hell."

I said, "I just want to know where the logic was in that."

He said, "Right is right. I was simply paying him back in kind. It was the only thing his kind could understand."

I said, "That's my point. You just don't go down there and go to paying back a bunch of rough hombres in kind. Or any other currency for that matter."

That made him look over at Dad. He said, "Dad, will you make him quit treating me like I was ten years old? He does it on purpose."

But he'd appealed to the wrong man. Dad just threw his hands in the air and aid, "Don't come to me with your troubles. I'm just a boarder around here. You get your orders from Justa. You know that."

Of course he didn't like that. Norris had always been a strong hand for the right and wrong of a matter. In fact, he may have been one of the most stubborn men I'd ever met. But he didn't say anything, just gave me a look and muttered something about hoping a mess came up at the bank while he was gone and then see how much boss I was.

But he didn't mean nothing by it. Like most families, we fought amongst ourselves and, like most families, God help the outsider who tried to interfere with one of us.

WESTERNS!

at least a savings of $3.00 each month below the publishers price. Second, there is never any shipping, handling or other hidden charges—Free home delivery. What's more there is no minimum number of books you must buy, you may return any selection for full credit and you can cancel your subscription at any time. A TRUE VALUE!

Mail the coupon below

To start your subscription and receive 2 FREE WESTERNS, fill out the coupon below and mail it today. We'll send your first shipment which includes 2 FREE BOOKS as soon as we receive it.

Mail To:
True Value Home Subscription Services, Inc.   10615
P.O. Box 5235
120 Brighton Road
Clifton, New Jersey 07015-5235

YES! I want to start receiving the very best Westerns being published today. Send me my first shipment of 6 Westerns for me to preview FREE for 10 days. If I decide to keep them, I'll pay for just 4 of the books at the low subscriber price of $2.45 each; a total of $9.80 (a $17.70 value). Then each month I'll receive the 6 newest and best Westerns to preview Free for 10 days. If I'm not satisfied I may return them within 10 days and owe nothing. Otherwise I'll be billed at the special low subscriber rate of $2.45 each; a total of $14.70 (at least a $17.70 value) and save $3.00 off the publishers price. There are never any shipping, handling or other hidden charges. I understand I am under no obligation to purchase any number of books and I can cancel my subscription at any time, no questions asked. In any case the 2 FREE books are mine to keep.

Name _____

Address _____ Apt. # _____

City _____ State _____ Zip _____

Telephone # _____

Signature _____
(if under 18 parent or guardian must sign)
Terms and prices subject to change.
Orders subject to acceptance by True Value Home Subscription Services, Inc.

J.R. ROBERTS
THE
GUNSMITH